Tears

WORDSWORTH ROMANCE

Tears

DENISE BRINIG

WORDSWORTH EDITIONS

The paper in this book is produced from pure wood pulp, without the use of chlorine or any other substance harmful to the environment. The energy used in its production consists almost entirely of hydroelectricity and heat generated from waste materials, thereby conserving fossil fuels and contributing little to the greenhouse effect.

First published by Macdonald Futura Publishers Limited

This edition published 1994 by
Wordsworth Editions Limited
Cumberland House, Crib Street, Ware,
Hertfordshire SG12 9ET

ISBN 1 85326 502 0

© Denise Brinig 1981

All rights reserved. This publication may not be reproduced, stored in a retrieval system, or transmitted, in any form or by any means, electronic, mechanical, photocopying, recording or otherwise without the prior permission of the publishers.

Printed and bound in Denmark by Nørhaven

To Shelley Power, my agent and friend, who told me that the duty of a writer is to be read.

Thanks to my daughter, Rebekah Brinig, for all her help, and to Marjory Chapman, my editor, for hers. Thanks too, to my friend Donald Rau, for his unfailing sense of humour and his very practical assistance with this book.

CHAPTER ONE

Cotton Joe's was jam-packed.

Placed as it was in a narrow alleyway within easy walking distance of most of the theatres in the labyrinth of Covent Garden, the restaurant was a perennial favourite with performing artists and the people around them.

The proprietor, an enormous, ancient, beaming Jamaican whose real name was Joseph Durer, had been an 'artiste' too in his time, or so he was fond of telling his regular patrons.

Whether it was true or not didn't matter. His place overflowed with opera singers in their seasons, ballet dancers in theirs, and with actors and actresses, musicians, stagehands, lighting staff, wardrobe personnel and ticket sellers all the year round.

The food he served was simple but dependably good, the prices modest, the service cheerful and fast.

Brief greetings were offered and acknowledged when Dominic Lautrec walked in with Anna Farnell. As they made their way to a table at the rear of the noisy, smoky room, the flow of lunchtime conversation closed behind them in their wake.

Anna was dressed casually, almost carelessly, in jeans and a faded red velour sweatshirt. Her blonde hair was caught at the nape of her neck in a ponytail, and she wore no make-up. She might have been fourteen, instead of twenty-two.

Dominic wore denim too, and a tee-shirt emblazoned

'I shot J.R.' in bold green letters. He was half a head taller than she, as dark as she was fair.

They made a handsome pair: young, slim, vital. It was obvious by the way he held her arm, by the way she laughed up at him, that they were in love. They might have been any couple pausing in their Saturday shopping for a lunchtime snack.

Almost anywhere else in London, they might have stopped traffic.

Anna Farnell's delicately beautiful face was known and adored by the ballet-loving public. Dominic Lautrec was equally well-known by the same public as the chivalrous Prince whose doomed romance resolves itself into a happy ending just in time for the final curtain.

At twenty-three, Dominic Lautrec was the youngest and most talented *danseur noble* the Company had ever yet cherished among its numbers, and he was Anna Farnell's partner. Even when they wore ordinary street clothes there was a sort of glow around them, and they generated an excitement when they moved together that was very nearly electric.

But Joe's was full of dancers that day, fellow members of the Royal Ballet who knew them as well as (or perhaps better than) they knew the members of their own families.

Dominic ordered omelettes, salads, white wine. As soon as the waiter turned away, he took up his argument where he had left it.

'Why do you doubt this, Anna?'

She smiled into his dark eyes, and shrugged.

'Because it's just gossip.'

Dominic heard it from one of the dressers, who said he had heard it from one of the principal teachers— Mikhail Niroff himself. The dry, diminutive Russian was scrupulous about his work, merciless in the use of his black dancing master's cane to point out the exact part of the foot, leg or body which the dancer must correct.

Outside class, Niroff was the communications centre of the Company grapevine.

Dominic grinned. 'Since when has the jungle telegraph been wrong?'

'Still—'

'Anna, it is only a matter of time before Steven tells us about this himself.'

'Perhaps. But even if it's true, he may refuse to release us—'

'Refuse to allow us to dance in Paris, in productions especially choreographed—that we inspired—and by Jean Lepage himself? Anna, Lepage is the most exciting choreographer in Europe!'

'Um. And Steven one of the most exacting of Company Directors.'

'Yes! But I can almost hear him now. He'll say: "No one is indispensable," in that slow, ponderous, measured tone of his, and off we'll go to France!'

Anna giggled at Dominic's exaggerated mimicry of Steven Harwood's clipped, aristocratic voice, at the characteristic chin-stroking gesture which almost invariably accompanied the Director's pronouncements—an impersonation made even funnier by the slight French intonation which Dominic hadn't completely lost after three years in England.

So far as any of them knew, Harwood's life was entirely centred on the Company, and he was universally respected for that. His dedication to it, his love for dance itself, had pulled them and shaped them into one of the largest and finest ballet companies in the world.

Not the least of his worries—always, relentlessly—was money: he would beg and plead for it, ferret it out and go on bended knee to get hold of it, to supplement the inflation-battered, constantly-threatened government subsidies which kept them going. The expenses of a production were never met by box-office receipts alone, not even a fraction of them.

Harwood watched box-office receipts too, of course. If he considered that the absence of two of the Company's most popular stars in any given season would seriously affect the number of tickets sold, he would decline to release them without a second thought.

The good of the Company came first; *esprit de corps* was more than just a phrase to Steven Harwood. It was his way of life.

'He might say we're not indispensable,' Anna conceded, tracing patterns on the scrubbed pine table with her fork. 'But then again he might not, and you know it. If he's planning a classical season for the autumn, he's sure to want us—'

'So much the better opportunity for him to point out that we are not the only principal dancers in the Company!'

The youngest, the most technically dazzling, the two who had captured the hearts of audiences and critics alike for the magic of their partnership, the elusive quality of genius which informed the roles they danced; but no, not the only principal dancers in the Company.

Dominic persisted. 'If this is true, and if Steven wants to produce *Sleeping Beauty* in the autumn, it would be a marvellous opportunity to cast Nicole as Aurora and Claude as the Prince. They've never danced it, and they've been with the Company longer than we have!'

Nicole Girard was twenty-five or twenty-six, a highly competent principal in the Company, technically sure and a good actress. Pretty as well, and just as hard-working and dedicated as Anna herself.

Poor Claude was competent too. And half in love with Nicole, though she seemed to take that very lightly.

Perhaps that was because Nicole's ambition left no time for love, or at least not for Claude Antonini.

A tiny, perplexed frown crossed Anna's face.

'You're not jealous, surely?' Dominic asked gently.

'Certainly I'm not! Why should I be?'

A dancer could be jealous of another. Everyone had heard stories of frustrated would-be stars stuffing broken glass into a rival's satin slippers, deliberately causing injury so that they themselves might appear on stage instead—though no one Anna knew had ever actually known anything like that to happen in real life.

A dancer's training was too rigorous to allow any time for such treacherous pettiness. More than that, such an action would betray the dignity bred into serious professionals along with the correct turn-out of the hip joints, the pointing of the feet.

The only real way to the top was to be the best, and everyone knew that too. And the highest praise Nicole or Claude had ever earned so far was 'highly competent'.

Anna reached out to take Dominic's hand, and her tone was soft. 'I'm sorry for snapping. But no, honestly, it's nothing like that. It's just—well—that the part of Aurora requires the girl to hold some of the most difficult and dramatic balances in the whole of the repertory. I just don't think Nicole's . . . ready for it.'

Dominic grinned and allowed himself an expressive Gallic shrug. 'But I think *we* are ready for Lepage, *chérie*. Don't you?'

The waiter brought wine and glasses. Dominic poured, and offered her a toast. Anna smiled as she raised her glass to his.

It was useless to argue against his enthusiasm, less than useless to spoil his pleasure. And if it were true . . .

If it were true that Jean Lepage had approached Steven Harwood with the request that they be released to dance a festival season in Paris, in which they would perform the Frenchman's interpretations of the classical roles which had skyrocketed them to fame in London, and *if* they were temporarily released from their contracts in order to do it, and *if* they were well-received in Lepage's productions, they might well be on their way to international stardom.

If, if, if . . .

It sounded too good to be true, all of it.

Both Anna's career and Dominic's, and theirs as a partnership, had been built in a dizzying progression of events, at a rate unprecedented within the formal, conservative, tradition-bound world of serious classical ballet.

And to dance their début as guest artists in the city where they had met, where they had worked together under Régine Barrère's strict, uncompromising guidance for one brutally exhausting but incomparably rewarding year, where their partnership had actually begun . . . that would complete a circle; it would seal their destinies.

CHAPTER TWO

Anna was eighteen in the spring she nearly didn't go to Paris.

She was living in Baron's Court, in a building which boasted an elegant late-Edwardian façade which was scrupulously maintained by frequent applications of twentieth-century paint.

Inside it had been partitioned into as many cubicles as possible, each carpeted and furnished on the cheap in the neutral tones of dried mud, equipped with small cookers operating off slot metres, and crammed with as many tenants as would fit.

Anna's place was really just one long, narrow room at the top of the house; its only grace note was the view through the dormer window of chimney-pots and sky.

The kitchen was a curtained alcove, the bath was on the landing, the furniture was predictably ugly and just adequate: a single bed which masqueraded as a sofa in the daytime, one small table flanked by two straight chairs, an armchair in front of a tiled fireplace in which an electric fire (also metred) was installed.

None of the rooms in the house was very different from any of the others. Not that anybody cared.

Most of the people who lived in them were students, nearing the end of seven or eight or ten years of concentrated, formal training which would fit them (they devoutly hoped) for careers on the professional ballet stage. Most, like Anna, were about to finish their graduate year at the Royal Ballet Upper School in Talgarth Road.

Their days invariably began early with warming-up class, with the *pliés* and *demi-pliés* which are as unchangeable as the order of the seasons, the daily message to muscles and ligaments and joints that demands are going to be made upon them. They were. For the rest of each day there would be more classes, in contemporary or character or regional dancing, in mime, dance notation, stage make-up.

There would be rehearsals of the Company's repertory too, to give the senior students the feeling of the complex *enchainements* of the steps of complete ballets.

If there was rivalry among the members of that enclosed, exclusive, dedicated world, there was a good deal of camaraderie as well.

At the quietest of times there were constant processions to laundry rooms in basements, where everlasting rows of washed and mended practise tights were no sooner dry than wet ones were hung their place.

In Anna's house, and in others very like it in the neighbourhood, coffee was usually going in somebody's room, and frequent impromptu parties were held; congratulations or commiserations were easily asked, and given.

It was a marvellous year for Anna.

First she was told she'd been chosen to dance the coveted starring role in the students' production of *Giselle* in the Annual Gala Performance at Covent Garden.

Martin and Helen Farnell came all the way down to London to watch her with uncritical, misty-eyed pride. Jason came too, of course, though even at eleven his childish hands were so twisted and swollen with arthritis he couldn't applaud his sister. That didn't stop him shouting 'Bravo!' at the top of his voice at every opportunity.

Anna's family couldn't know that her feet felt frozen, her smile false, or that in the second act—when she was meant to be dancing her lover to death—each graceful *arabesque* brought with it the fear that she might slip and fall and make a fool of herself.

She didn't. Weeks later, when she was picked to 'cover' for a member of the *corps* in a professional performance of *La Bayadère*, the honour was greater still.

Anna was plunged into the difficult minor role almost without warning, when the girl whose understudy she was became ill, and remained ill through the première and for four performances after it.

Finally, Anna was offered a place of her own in the *corps de ballet*.

Put so, such an offer sounds a disappointment, as though her talent had been dismissed as second-rate, her dancing found wanting.

Nothing was further from the truth.

There is fierce and passionate competition among young dancers to fix their *pointe* shoes onto that particular rung of the long ladder to stardom as soloists and principal dancers, and the duration of any dancer's presence in a *corps* is very flexible.

Some *corps* members remain there all their dancing lives, contributing to the unity and perfection without which classical ballet would be a sparse and barren enterprise. Others, fewer and further between—driven by talent, ambition, luck and hard work in roughly equal quantities—are promoted sooner or later into the limelight of centre stage.

The offer of the place was Anna's first genuine triumph as a professional dancer; she was thrilled with it.

She had worked for it, of course. So had all the dancers and aspiring dancers with whom she studied.

The testing time for girls comes when they first learn to dance on the tips of their toes, usually when they are twelve years old, never before the feet and legs are strong enough to make it safely possible.

The mastery of the ability to float across a stage *sur les pointes* is a painful task, a labour of love and determination which effectively separates those who are serious about a career in classical ballet from those who are not.

Toes were not designed to take the entire weight of the human body, no matter how slender and elegantly proportioned it may be. The achievement is paid for in an agony of sore feet and blisters, turned ankles, occasional falls.

That is just the beginning. Afterwards there are countless hours of patient struggles to correct weakness in line, in temperament, in acting ability; years spent honing and perfecting the dancer's only tool: the human body.

Comparatively few last the course; fewer still receive the offer of a real, honest-to-God paying job at the end of it.

Anna was about to accept, but she had reckoned without Régine Barrère. Half-French, half-Russian, the ageing *ballerina assoluta* was one of the last living dancers from Diaghilev's Ballet Russe who had fled the Russian Revolution to live and work in Paris.

Her first interview with Anna was conducted in the chaos of a dressing room in Talgarth Road, directly after morning class. Most of the girls there were semi-nude, quite unselfconscious as they flung leg-warmers and tights in every direction in their haste to struggle into street clothes and out to the hurried lunches which would stoke them for the afternoon's rehearsals. They were cheerfully at ease confiding news of boyfriends and as people to whom Régine Barrère's name was a household word.

Anna had changed them. Anna at seven, hop-skipping joyously in her white hair ribbon and ruffled pinafore dress at her recital of what she had learned in a local beginners' ballet class; Anna at eleven, leaving home to go to boarding school in Richmond when her dancing teacher in Pendleton recommended she be entered for auditions there; Anna at eighteen, so pretty, so talented, so wonderfully happy; Anna dancing, always dancing—that fateful summer dancing off to Paris.

It was arranged as though by magic, the *corps* declined with grateful thanks, and Anna's ticket booked.

She could remember it clearly ever afterwards, her first sight of Régine Barrère's studio: the piano hulking in one corner, the rigid cluster of hard, straight-backed chairs beside it, and of course the mirrors and the *barre*.

It was her heaven and her hell, a test beyond anything which had gone before it; the proving ground for a handful of dancers who had received the *imprimatur* of Barrère's unerring instinct for genius.

CHAPTER THREE

Anna met Dominic there. Her first impression of him was one she was fond of telling him sometimes, just to watch his reaction.

'I thought you were a footballer.'

He never failed to find that funny. 'Better that,' he would say, 'than a ballet boy, *dearie*.' The 'dearie' went with a high camp, limp-wristed gesture. Dominic imagined a widespread public suspicion that all male ballet dancers were queer.

'No one ever accused you of that!' she would gasp, pretending to be horrified.

Actually, it had never occurred to her.

It had probably never occurred to any woman, and if any man had ever questioned Dominic's sexual preference, the sight of his lean, athletic and visibly powerful body had prevented the question being asked aloud.

Dominic was born to be a *danseur noble*, a title which means exactly what it sounds like: a noble male dancer. Tough, electric, supportive, strong.

He was tall, an inch or so below six feet; he was good-looking too, a convincing Prince Charming with dark curling hair and brown eyes. Velvet eyes, Anna said.

Before Régine Barrère had picked him out of a student production of Tennessee Williams' *Streetcar Named Desire*—in which he was cast as the *macho* Stanley Kowalski—Dominic had received little if any training as a dancer. His father, dead when Dominic was fourteen, had wanted him to be a doctor; his mother, happily remarried and living near Limoges, wanted merely Dominic's happiness. When he telephoned her to ask what he should do, she told him to follow his heart.

So Madame persuaded Dominic to leave the University of Paris, where he was struggling indifferently through his first year, and come to her instead. He accepted her offer of free, intensive tuition with a 'what the hell' gesture, a slightly embarrassed shrug which didn't quite hide the excitement in his eyes.

It was only by the grace of his having done gymnastics at school that he was remotely fit to learn what the old woman could teach him. Within months, he had made up for years of lost time.

Anna realized that the first time he lifted her. She couldn't see him, but she could feel the firm pressure of his hands below her ribs, and her muscles tautened.

'Allez-hop! *And* up!'

Her toes pushed her off the floor, high, easy, carried still higher by his arms. Oh God, she had never before been lifted with the sureness, the strength, the perfection. He held her weightless in the air without strain, dream-easy, dream-beautiful.

Their first date, coming later, seemed almost anticlimactic, their intimacy already established in their work. By then they felt they had been working together most of their lives. Of Barrère's handful of flawless dancers, Anna and Dominic were easily the finest, a fact the old ballerina recognized by working them harder than anybody else.

Her small group existed on the generosity of its patrons combined with economies Barrère effected by renting small, shabby theatres for their performances, and by watching all the expenses of production like a hawk.

It was impossible for her to stage lavish, full-length ballets; even if she could have found the money, there were too few dancers in the group for that. Instead her repertory consisted of carefully-chosen excerpts from long works, and new pieces which focused and emphasized the talents of the soloist to the greatest extent possible.

Barrère demanded perfection from her dancers. With her finest successes, she achieved all the elegance and aristocracy of line her own Russian training had instilled in her.

It was said with truth that when a dancer finished studying with Barrère, he or she could dance anywhere in the world.

Anna's first date with Dominic began casually, a coffee shared in a bistro after a strenuous rehearsal. But because even then he felt limitlessly wealthy in her presence, he put her into a taxi and took her out to the Bois de Boulogne to eat in a restaurant under glass chandeliers suspended from trees.

He ordered trout and wine, and later they took a walk and watched the ladies and gentlemen cantering along the bridle paths as though nothing had happened since 1870.

The two were together often; very soon after that first shared summer's evening, they were inseparable.

Dominic was older than Anna, though only by a year. It might have been several, reckoned in terms of his wider knowledge of the world. He was determined to take his time, to be sure of her feelings and his own before their involvement became serious, sexual.

One evening he asked, 'Have you ever been in love?'

'Oh yes, when I was nine. He was thirteen and he lived next door but one.' Anna laughed at the memory. 'He had a paper round early in the morning, and I used to get up hours before I had to go to school, to stand at my bedroom window and watch him leave on his bicycle.'

'And since?'

She considered that. 'I don't think so. All I ever really wanted to do was to dance, and . . . the two don't seem to mix very well.'

'They might, Anna, if you fell in love with me, for instance.'

They were walking at dusk along a grand boulevard rich with trees. Anna stopped and looked up at him gravely, and then he bent to kiss her mouth for the first time.

Dominic lived in two impossibly tiny rooms, accessible only to the very young or the very nimble by climbing flights and flights of narrow wooden stairs.

He and Anna made love there, and after that nothing mattered at all except that they were together. Their lives became inextricably woven, one with the other, and both dedicated to dancing.

Either would have been startled, had they stopped to think of it, that at least some part of the atmosphere they were able to create on stage was their ability to convince an audience—quite effortlessly, as it was true—that they were lovers in 'real' life.

Where dancing left off, and 'real' life began, neither could have said.

The year flew by and summer came again. Anna wanted to go back to London, to audition for the Royal Ballet, to try her wings in the largest, most prestigious company in the world.

'Well, you are ready now,' Madame said.

By then it was unthinkable that Dominic remain behind, or that Anna go without him.

Régine Barrère smiled her thoughtful, knowing approval.

'You are ready as well, Dominic. And I think . . . that

together you may well build a partnership to dazzle the world.'

Dominic took Anna to Limoges to meet his mother.

'I want her to know why I'm leaving France, and to know how happy I am to have found you.'

'She'll ask—'

'Why we don't marry?'

Anna nodded, shy, and Dominic drew her close. He kissed her hair.

'Will you marry me, Anna?'

'Oh yes, of course I will! But not now! Not until—'

'Yes.' He grinned. 'My mother is sufficiently unconventional to be able to understand that. You'll see.'

She did. Marie Lautrec-Ravel was a slim, smiling woman who looked like a pocket edition of her handsome son. She liked Anna on sight, and made much of her, rejoicing in lyrical, silvery laughter that two working dancers could afford to eat the rich, fine foods she loved to cook without worrying about losing their cat-like slimness.

Helen and Martin Farnell were rather less understanding, even slightly alarmed at first to hear of Anna's and Dominic's decision to live together in London.

'Are you sure that's what you want, dear?' Helen asked hesitantly in her soft country voice when Anna rang her from Heathrow.

'Yes, mum. Wait until you've met him. We're so happy together, so very happy. It's just not time for us to marry, that's all.'

When Anna brought Dominic to Pendleton for the first time, the Farnells were disarmed, but only by degrees.

Helen was charmed by his deferential courtesy at once, perhaps by the flowers he remembered to buy at King's Cross before he and Anna started out.

Martin was quiet, warily reserved, right through the

ritual pre-Sunday-lunch sherry and the good, plain English meal which followed.

When it was finished he sat back in his chair and regarded the young pair seriously.

'I can see you're fond of one another,' he said, 'and though I'm not a worldly man, I'm not so old-fashioned I can't understand why you might want to delay marrying. It seems the way of many young people these days, though I daresay some seem to undertake the arrangement with a lot less thought than you've brought to it. I'll not stand in your way. And Dominic,' he finished formally, 'you're to consider yourself very welcome here. One of the family.'

And then Martin smiled his slow, sweet smile and offered Dominic a cigar, and everyone relaxed.

Jason adored Dominic without reservation from the moment he walked through the door. Dominic had the good sense to be in love with his big sister and besides, he was the first real live Frenchman Jason had ever met.

Anna and Dominic were accepted into the Royal Ballet *corps* almost immediately after their auditions, and promoted out of it into *coryphée* status within a month. Within a year they were soloists. Within three, they were principal dancers.

Their partnership was established when the critics labelled it 'indescribably moving', and 'a triumph of art over the dull greys of workaday gravity', to watch them dance together.

Two days after their début as principals in *Swan Lake*, Dominic sat tailor-fashion on the sofa in their living-room, reading aloud to Anna from *The Sunday Times*.

'...*Miss Farnell's execution of the bourrée steps at the end of Act II created the illusion that she was actually floating across the stage as the Swan Queen, Odette.*

'By superb contrast, her fiery control as the dazzling, evil Odile in Act III sent shivers down my spine. Such technical brilliance, such a range of talent in any dancer's performance as Odette/Odile is a rare treat. In one so very young—Anna Farnell is barely twenty-two—'

'Only just,' Anna interrupted in a dazed whisper, fingering the delicate golden chain at her neck which had been Dominic's birthday gift.

'—the quality of her talent is unlikely to be rivalled in her lifetime. What is even more unlikely—'

There Dominic let the paper fall from his hands as he clapped a palm to his head and began to babble in French.

'Well?' Anna held her breath.

Dominic looked up at her, blinking. 'There is more,' he said.

She laughed. 'Well naturally there is, twit! They hadn't even got to you yet. Come on, carry on reading!'

Dominic retrieved the paper and scanned the piece to find his place.

'—even more unlikely is that Miss Farnell was partnered by Dominic Lautrec, a French-born dancer who is her senior by less than a year, in a performance as Siegfried which was equally flawless and as seemingly effortless as her own.'

'Dominic, I think—I think they liked us.'

'What was your first clue? They go on and on for paragraphs!'

'They . . . do?'

They did. There was a piece in the *Observer* as well, and another in the *Telegraph*.

In the months that followed every performance in which Dominic partnered Anna was sold out.

The critics surpassed themselves; superlative upon superlative was set into type like so many bouquets of roses until it seemed that all the words of highest praise were used up. When the critics had exhausted their stock completely they settled for comparing Anna to Taglioni, to Pavlova, and Dominic to Nijinsky.

The effect of success on the Farnell/Lautrec partnership was to make them work harder, and harder still.

Perhaps it *was* possible that Jean Lepage had seen them dance, that he had remarked their growing fame, that he had decided to choreograph productions around them, showcases for their brilliance, as well as his own.

When Steven Harwood confirmed the rumour, late in the afternoon on the day Dominic told Anna of it, and when he gave his grave, considered permission for them to accept Lepage's invitation, Anna burst into tears of joy.

The following day she heard (via Dominic, via Mikhail Niroff) that indeed Steven *was* planning to rehearse Nicole and Claude in *The Sleeping Beauty* as part of his autumn season.

Anna smiled, really smiled. Nicole deserved the chance.

CHAPTER FOUR

There was a time when Pendleton was just another sleepy provincial town in the gently undulating Buckinghamshire countryside, and Daniel Rogerson the only doctor within a radius of ten miles.

He practised from the brick cottage in Pendleton High Street which had been both surgery and home to him since the day he arrived from Leicester with his general practitioner's licence at the age of twenty-four.

His was a good career, unremarkable perhaps, and certainly unsung, but in many ways a great deal more demanding than that of a big-city doctor with everything modern easily to hand.

He'd had his share of problems; not the least of them was the fact that his semi-rural practice was conducted many miles from the nearest general hospital. Even patients in a semi-rural area sometimes required to be taken to hospital, some in more of a hurry than others: the acutely ill, the accident victims, the dying who might be saved by a specialist's care.

For the rest, Daniel coped well. A measure of his competence and caring was that in all his years of practice he had managed (with the help of two midwives and a splendid district nurse) to bring the majority of his patients into the world and through the usual hazards of childhood to a healthy maturity, and to do the same for their children.

Martin Farnell's people were among Daniel's first patients: the senior Farnells, Martin himself, his married sisters and their growing families.

When Martin met plump, fair, laughing Helen Prowse at a dance in the market town where he studied accountancy, fell in love with her and married her, Daniel (self-confessed confirmed bachelor that he was) came to their wedding and kissed the bride.

Daniel personally assisted Anna into the world, and seven years later Jason as well. He was there to monitor their healthy babyhoods, to shepherd each of them safely through mumps and chicken pox and measles, to rejoice with Helen and Martin—though there was sadness too on that occasion—when the eleven-year-old Anna was chosen to go to the ballet boarding school in London.

When Jason was seven, Helen sent for Daniel urgently because the child was running a high fever and complaining of pains in his knees.

'It isn't polio, is it Dan?' she whispered, frightened, when they had left the little boy sleeping peacefully, comforted by the gruff, familiar teasing and the big, shiny stethoscope.

'Oh Helen no, it's nothing like that! You've got to calm yourself, or you'll be ill as well,' he added gently, patting her arm.

Jason had been properly immunized and besides, Daniel hadn't heard of or seen a case of infantile paralysis in the county for over twenty years. And he'd seen enough of it in his early days of practice to know it wasn't that.

Daniel thought it just might be rheumatic fever, though he didn't say so; he'd seen enough of that, too, to suspect it wasn't likely.

'Helen, I don't honestly know what's the matter. Not yet. I'll call in to look at him again this evening. If he wakes in pain, give him a crushed aspirin in sugar water, and above all, keep him in bed.'

Daniel Rogerson was a country doctor, scrupulously

careful because he had to be and because he really cared. He was respectfully aware of the diagnostic possibilities yielded by the modest but very up-to-date laboratory, as well-equipped as his health service budget and his personal finances had allowed, in the rooms behind his surgery.

He ran tests on Jason's blood himself; the results were in Jason's notes, recorded as exhaustively as possible. His diagnosis was: 'Juvenile arthritis. Still's disease,' with a circled question mark.

Daniel requested an appointment for Jason to be seen by a consultant rheumatologist in a Birmingham hospital.

The consultant's diagnosis, when it finally came, more or less confirmed Daniel's. Jason's illness was, after all, classifiable as 'rheumatoid arthritis'. Whether or not the condition would disappear as he grew older was unknown, unknowable.

The reason for that was technical: hospital tests on Jason's blood revealed the presence of what the doctors called IgM rheumatoid factor, and the outlook for his complete recovery was rather worse than it would have been if they had not.

'Will he grow out of it?' Martin asked.

'It's impossible to say,' Daniel answered. 'He may, and then again, he may not. But we'll have him swimming, and exercising, and as active as possible in every way.'

Meanwhile Jason grew, a blond miniature of his sister. He was ill sometimes, with fever and swollen joints, but that didn't appear to affect his popularity at school or his academic progress.

Jason wanted to study law, he said, and he showed every sign of being capable of that. And he was keenly interested in his sister's career. 'She'll dance for both of us,' he said sometimes, grinning proudly.

When Jason was twelve (and Anna nineteen, and dancing with Régine Barrère in Paris) the new town of Elmwood Centre was designated by Parliament.

Pendleton found itself just within the southern boundary of the 35,000-acre site, suddenly included by law in a sprawling maze of new housing estates designed to accommodate the 'urban overspill' of city families who came to swell the original population of the area by more than double in the first year of its existence.

The old-timers called it 'The Year of the Bulldozers'.

Daniel Rogerson felt himself too old at sixty-three to cope with the mushrooming demands of Elmwood's four new aluminium and clapboard temporary health centres, its twenty-five-bed day hospital, or with the supervision of the several young and earnest general practitioners who were taken on to assist him.

He resigned as senior general practitioner after six months of punishing hard work which resulted, his colleagues in Birmingham assured him, in his first heart attack, and James Harrington was hired to take his place.

James was a tall man, broad-shouldered and slow-moving, with deep-set grey eyes and big, gentle hands, a man who inspired confidence just to look at him. At thirty-five he was young enough, strong enough, optimistic enough about the eventual prospects for adequate health care facilities in the fledgling new town to be glad to be part of it.

By that time Elmwood had attracted enough industry to be able to fill most of its rows and rows of ugly, jerry-built houses; by that time the health centres were permanently and hopelessly full, in hours and out of hours, of patients whose illnesses were real or imagined or sometimes both, depending upon the doctor's point of view and his degree of tiredness.

James was lonely in the first few months, overworked and dispirited by the sheer weight of the case load he and his young colleagues were expected to handle.

He was battling in most of his precious 'free' time too, to persuade anyone influential who would listen that he needed more doctors, more equipment, more space; above all, that Elmwood Centre needed a hospital of its own.

The waiting lists for hospital consultations and admissions had grown out of all proportion to the number of consultants and beds available in Birmingham. So James coined a slogan which a local printer made up into bumper stickers and posters for any window whose owner was willing to display it: 'Elmwood Centre is dying for a hospital'.

In a way, the job was what James Harrington had wanted: so demanding he had no time to think about himself at all, no time to remember the busy practice he had left behind in Yorkshire or the young wife he had buried there beside their stillborn child.

No one knew about any of that; no one appeared to notice that Dr Harrington might have come from somewhere else, or left some other life behind him.

It was a relief that most of the patients he saw were so full of their own miseries they couldn't see the doctor as a human being at all. In another way, it was a relief when he realized he had inherited the friendship of the Farnell family along with the responsibility for Jason's care.

'You ought to come for lunch with us one Sunday when you're free, Dr Harrington. That is,' Helen amended with an embarrassed laugh, 'if you ever are.'

James was embarrassed too. He had just examined Jason Farnell; he had just prescribed, without much real hope, yet another anti-inflammatory drug which might or might not work better than the last one had to bring the boy's swollen wrists to a normal, painless size.

A part of his medical training and his own temperament and the very real remnants of his personal grief told him to keep his distance, not to become involved with any of his patients or their families on a personal level.

But then he remembered what Daniel Rogerson had said about the Farnells.

'The boy's not what you'd expect with his history. He's bright, cheeky, interested. More . . .' Daniel thought for a moment. '. . . more accepting than resigned to his condition, if you see what I mean. There's no doubt his parents and his older sister are largely to thank for that. He adores Anna, by the way. It's almost as though she's doing for both of them what he can't do for himself. She's in London, studying to be a ballet dancer, and Jason thinks the southern moon shines out of her satin slippers. You ought to get to know them, James. You'll not be sorry.'

So James said, 'Thank you, Mrs Farnell. I'd like to come.' And he had not been sorry.

Over the years James enjoyed the company of the Farnells as much as they enjoyed his; he looked forward to the Sunday lunches Helen cooked, the comfortable serenity of the family who shared them, the talk of Anna, and above all the satisfaction of seeing Jason's determined progress into maturity despite the frequent bouts of pain and disability.

In Dominic's honour Helen created *coq au vin* out of what would normally have been roast chicken. She served it with potatoes *à la gratin dauphinoise* made with Gruyère cheese which Anna brought specially from London, and to go with it all she served *petits pois* cooked with lettuce and onions and fresh mint.

It was all very French, very satisfying, though the entire menu had been rendered faithfully from Helen's dependable chain store all-colour cookery book. Even the ultra-conservative Martin pronounced it very good indeed.

Dominic, raised on the unshakeable notion that fine food deserves a fine wine, brought champagne.

'Champagne can be served with anything,' he said to Anna, 'and there's really no other wine so very festive.'

'Or so expensive,' Anna supplied, not really caring, grinning wickedly.

Dominic shook his head and smiled at her, traced her smiling mouth with a finger tip. 'How often do the stars collide in such great bounty?'

Jason's fifteenth birthday was on the Thursday of that week. Just one week earlier to the day, Elmwood Centre Community Hospital had been formally dedicated by a minor but nonetheless Royal personage.

Anna and Dominic were about to leave for Paris, for two months of close rehearsal with Lepage and the Paris Opera Ballet Company which would precede their début in *Swan Lake*, early in September.

Toasts were offered at the Farnells' large, round table that Sunday. Martin's was the first:

'To Paris! To international fame and—and to—to happiness for all of us.'

He sat down again quite quickly and flushed a little, self-conscious over his uncharacteristic attempt at showmanship. But Jason applauded, and James Harrington beamed.

Jason had recently been examined by a consultant at the new hospital, and a sophisticated new treatment had begun. Though nothing was said of it that afternoon, for the first time in many years Jason could enjoy the complete absence of pain; he could applaud. The treatment was working.

Dominic rose, gesturing to Anna that she should rise beside him. Together they executed the traditional *reverence* of thanks for Martin's toast. Dominic offered another.

'Happiness for all of us.'

James offered, 'To health, wealth and wisdom . . . and to happiness.'

It was a happy afternoon, with the June sunlight streaming in at the window and the shared meal a sacrament of love and hope and laughter.

CHAPTER FIVE

'Ladies, you are swans, if you please. Swans, not baby elephants! See? *Pas de chat, pas de chat, pas de chat,* so!'

Jean Lepage demonstrated the delicate precision he expected from the four *coryphées* at the beginning of Act II, *Swan Lake*: the steps of the cat.

'So!' He finished, and smiled disarmingly at the exhausted young dancers. 'This piece has no real meaning or relevance to the story, but remember: it will stop the show. We wish to get it just so, eh? Once again, ladies, please.'

Lepage could, and frequently did, take any role in any of the works they were rehearsing and dance it flawlessly himself. He never demanded of any dancer a step or sequence which he himself hadn't fully analyzed and understood; that was part of his charm, one of the reasons for his enormous popularity. Indeed he was a great dancer, and had been for years before he established himself as a choreographer.

His own career had begun in Paris, in the very Company where he was an honoured visitor for his Festival. The dancers of the Opera Ballet Company and all their magnificent facilities were at his disposal.

The Festival was privately and generously funded, and already Parisian balletomanes were queueing excitedly to obtain tickets—any ticket for any performance, in any available seat in the house—for the month-long Gala.

When it was finished Lepage would disappear into secluded 'retirement' in his large, rambling house on the outskirts of Paris until he was ready with the next one. It wouldn't necessarily be produced in France. With Lepage's fame, his reputation for professionalism, and his enduring popularity with the ballet-going public, it might be anywhere in the world.

The man was forty-one, though with his great shock of prematurely white hair and the energy of a boy, he could have been any age at all. Tall, slender, faultlessly graceful, Lepage was tireless in his insistence on perfection in every aspect of the works he created. But always, he was most demanding of himself.

His streamlined yet unabashedly lavish production of *Swan Lake* was his special pride, the masterpiece of his current season.

The original work had suffered a chequered history following its Russian conception, a series of choppings and changings which eventually resulted in its being dropped from the Bolshoi repertory in 1877.

Tchaikovsky himself was largely responsible for its revival in 1895, and the inspired choreography of Marius Petipa and Lev Ivanov for its brilliant success.

Lepage followed the Russians' work with meticulous care; his changes were deft and sensitive, and served merely to focus most of the audience's attention on the gifted pair who were to dance the central characters. To do that he shortened the third act by leaving out two national dances, and substituted them with an even more spectacular part for Anna Farnell, a tortuously demanding solo which required her to perform the feared and celebrated *fouetté* step as the wicked Odile not thirty-two times as in the Petipa version, but thirty-four.

'Two more, you see? For luck, dear Anna.'

'Jean, I'm not at all sure I can—'

'Nonsense, my dear, of course you can! You'll be famous for it!'

Thirty-four whipping turns executed on one leg, on one spot. It was a magnificent *tour de force*, some would say a circus trick. But it worked. The first time Anna performed it in full dress rehearsal, the orchestra stood as one man to applaud her.

In addition to *Swan Lake*, Lepage would produce *Les Sylphides*, in which he had made only minor changes but for which he had designed several *pas de deux variations* to follow it. He would also present Jules Perrot's original choreography of *Giselle* in which he had made virtually no changes at all.

The season was intended to evoke the haunting beauty of a world of sheer, lyrical romance, a fairy-tale realm of ethereal make-believe which the Farnell/Lautrec partnership would bring wonderfully to life.

It was a major departure for Lepage, or at least it would seem so to the critics, his working so faithfully and carefully within the classical traditions.

He had made his most spectacular reputation as a choreographer of *avant garde* works in which he used the angular techniques of modern dance and contemporary rhythms to startling effect; his major work had been called a new genre within ballet, and the best of it was energetic, light-hearted, even comical.

'At the heart of the matter, however,' he was frequently heard to say, 'there is the duty to maintain as much range as possible, and to use the materials one is given in the appropriate way—to surprise one's audience, to give them true delight!'

To this end he was prepared to supervise every aspect of production. He was with the painters on the sets he had commissioned, or with the wardrobe staff, the musicians, the conductor, the electricians, and naturally most often with the dancers themselves, coaxing them, bullying them, praising them, until they could give him the standard of performance he was determined to present.

So rehearsals continued through sweltering July and into stifling August until it sometimes seemed that each member of the Company was living, breathing, eating and sleeping dance.

It seemed too as though Lepage himself had no other life, no interest in anything apart from his work.

It wasn't so. Several weeks after rehearsals had begun in furious earnest, a strikingly lovely brunette appeared in the rehearsal hall one afternoon, leading two round-eyed, serious looking little boys by the hands.

The three of them sat quietly in hard-backed chairs until Lepage led them forward and introduced the woman as his wife, and the boys as their sons.

'And tomorrow, as a reward for very hard work, I should like to declare a holiday. My family and I would be very pleased if you will join us for a picnic in the Parc Monceau.'

'Ovaltine and Agatha Christie would be more like it,' Anna said later, when she and Dominic were walking along the Rue de Seine in search of supper, on the way back to their hotel. He stopped and turned to face her, twisted a strand of her hair playfully around one finger while he bent to kiss her.

'You sound like an old, old woman,' he teased. 'You are young and strong, in Paris, on the verge of a success, and I hope in love with me. What could be gayer than a picnic with Lepage and his charming family?'

'Ovaltine and Agatha Christie. I already told you.' She made a face at him. 'The man's been working us to death.'

It was an exaggeration, but like most exaggerations it contained a kernel of truth. They were all overworked, but none more so than Dominic and Anna.

Les Sylphides is one of the few survivors of Diaghilev's early productions. It is a ballet of mood, sometimes happy, sometimes nostalgic, but always extremely difficult to perform well because it demands so much more than mere technique. The ghosts of Pavlova, Karsavina and Nijinsky still haunt the work, and it is awe-inspiring to try to live up to the legends.

As for *Giselle*, though the pair had danced it many times in London, it was still a fresh, daunting challenge, particularly in acting skill.

Lepage kept insisting that in her 'mad' scene at the end of Act I, when Giselle dies in her mother's arms, Anna's portrayal must be prevented at all costs from descending into coyness.

'Giselle is *mad*, Anna, truly unseated in her reason. You must grimace, so, and you must relive your love for Count Albrecht with clear, poignant, heart-rending gestures and expressions. You must look into the character, into the depths of her unhappiness. You must make me *believe* in her tragedy!

'And *you*, Dominic! My God, the poor girl is dying before your eyes! You must do more than pretend to horror. You must feel it! You are responsible for it, after all.'

Most demanding of all, as it would be their première performance and the longest of the three works, the centre-piece of the festival and its choreography largely of Lepage's own devising, was *Swan Lake*.

'It is impossible, Jean, this trick you demand of Odile, that she should perform thirty-four of these wickedly difficult *pirouettes* and still remain upright!'

'No, no, dear Anna, it is not impossible for you,' he said. 'I have designed the sequence for you personally, and you shall be an international star because of it. Now once more, please, and this time allow me to see the icy, scheming treachery of Odile's smile as she hoodwinks

Prince Siegfried into believing she is his beloved Odette.'

Apart from the work in rehearsal there were costume fittings, for Lepage would have none of the standard wardrobe stock from the Opera's existing supply. 'These tattered grey affairs look as though they've been in use since the war!' he cried on one occasion. Fairly, since some of them had.

There were photographic sessions for the advance publicity (in costumes pinned and tacked because they weren't yet finished, probably wouldn't be completely finished before the evening of the première); there were interviews with the Parisian press, and always there was more work, and yet more work.

There were disasters as well, inevitable in such an ambitious project involving so many people; it seemed once or twice as though they would defeat even the indefatigable Jean Lepage in his dream of a perfect festival.

One of the girls who was to dance the *pas de quatre* of little swans in *Swan Lake* sprained her ankle badly and had to be replaced by a less experienced dancer, who had to endure Lepage's strained patience as she was inducted into the precise, difficult role.

Someone else managed to catch a hellish summer cold and pass it along to most of the members of the *corps de ballet*, resulting in peasant scenes in which there was far more sneezing than the required gaiety.

Dozens and dozens of pairs of satin slippers were utterly ruined when a careless deliveryman left them overnight in his van, and it rained.

With all that there was laughter ringing continually in the air; the overwhelming atmosphere was one of privilege at being able to work together, and of great excitement.

There was rest too, of course, at the end of the long,

hot days. Even for Anna and Dominic.

They had taken a hotel room in the Place Dauphin, a double—after the mildest of lifted eyebrows from the elderly *concierge*. The room was unpretentious but clean, with great pots of flowers lined up along the whitewashed windowsill, and a view of a small park.

Except for *croissants* and superb coffee served early each morning, the hotel supplied no meals at all. That was an advantage. It meant that they could unwind, wandering around each evening at dusk, choosing first one and then another of the cafés and bistros and brasseries which they had frequented during the first days of their courtship.

Anna could indulge her passion for good Alsatian *choucroute* and steaming *potages* and lobster sandwiches rich with mayonnaise.

Once in a while, for sentimental reasons, Dominic would take her back to the Bois to the restaurant where they had shared their first meal.

'Sometimes it seems that all we do is eat,' Dominic mused one evening. 'In our free time, I mean.'

Anna fixed him with a long, loving look. 'Not quite,' she murmured. Then she sighed deeply. 'What free time? We're working our guts out for that depraved perfectionist.'

Dominic shook his head and smiled at her, poured more wine. 'Darling, he's doing it for us as well. It will be the making of us, you'll see.'

They talked seriously of that for a time, their careers, their incredible good luck; then, through the echoing night streets of Paris, beneath a moon which silvered their hair and made their faces seem to glow, they walked slowly back to their hotel.

Tears

It was done. It had been jolly and gay and satisfyingly sentimental, very effective in the huge, elaborate theatre. But at last the lights were down and the curtain rising again; this time the orchestra struck the opening chords of Tchaikovsky's score and on stage it was Prince Siegfried's birthday, and Dominic had begun to dance.

Anna watched, and though she had stood watching the same scene unfolding countless times before, she watched in fresh amazement, caught up in the suspension of disbelief, the excitement of it all, as much as any member of the audience might be.

She knew by then what she would experience, and in what order, before her own appearance. Just before her entrance into the lakeside-by-moonlight scene in Act II, she would be totally convinced that the ribbons of her slippers had come undone. She would turn with a startled cry of 'Oh my God!' to one of the plump, middle-aged Frenchwomen who worked as dressers. Knowing her, knowing dancers, whoever it was she turned to would smile.

The woman would bend quickly to check, to make doubly sure, and then she would kiss Anna's cheek, flushed beneath her make-up. 'No, no, *petite*, it is secure. Go now, and fly!'

The next stage of panic was the worst of all, but at least it would be the last one. Anna would feel as though her feet were weighted with lead, that she could not move them. And as suddenly as the feeling had come, it would leave her.

Then she would fly.

It would feel as marvellous as it would look, and it would make every moment of struggle and agony and sweat and bad temper and frustration worthwhile.

Anna would *be* the Swan Maiden, trembling on the

stage, and when Dominic raised her in his strong, sure arms she would fall in love with him all over again in the impossible, exquisitely perfect dream of it all. She wouldn't pause again for worry or for any conscious thought. She had absorbed it all and digested it in the very depths of her soul.

By turn she would be the gentle Odette, the brittle and grasping Odile with her impossibly difficult solo, and then Odette again, soaring in mid-air in Dominic's expert, confident lifts, and at the end of it she would be in love with him, and he with her, throughout eternity. Curtain.

Strangely to her, when she thought about it, the whole thing would seem to be over in a flash of seconds, all the hard work of it, and all of Dominic's as well—his complete, masterful accuracy in his *jetés*, his lifts, his control while they seemed to hover on the stage as he held her aloft and she made pretty *batteries* in mid-air.

The applause, the flowers that came afterwards always came as a delightful surprise.

After that there would be a party, or supper at least, perhaps praise; 'reality', whatever that might be.

'We work so hard at this it's—*programmed* into us,' Dominic said when she mentioned it to him. 'It only seems like a flash of seconds. But I understand, I feel the same about it. Shall we eat now?'

Always that. And then the winding down, the coming out of the strenuous dream together, holding one another close, making love, and then the next day's rehearsal: an idyllic life.

'Miss Farnell?'

'Shh! Please—'

'Miss Farnell, I am very sorry, but I must speak to you.'

Tears

Dominic/Siegfried was dancing his melancholy solo, unhappy with his mother's insistence that he must marry, expressing his disappointment with the six maidens she had chosen as his bridal candidates; it was moving, beautifully done.

Very soon he would be interrupted, persuaded to accompany his courtiers on a swan hunt. Very soon he would discover Odette in the forest—

'Miss Farnell, I beg of you!'

'What—what is it, Berthe?'

'It is a telegram from England, Miss Farnell. It is marked "urgent". I am so very sorry.'

Anna regarded the woman and blinked rapidly, shocked out of her reverie. 'A telegram? From whom?'

'From England, Miss Farnell. I am so very sorry. They said you must read it at the first possible moment, I—'

'Oh Berthe, you couldn't help it. I'm sorry for snapping at you!'

'I understand, Miss Farnell. I wish it could have been anyone else to bring this.'

To break into this tortuous Anglo-French minuet of courtesy, Anna held out her hand for the coarse envelope; with one eye on the stage, she ripped it open impatiently.

A telegram from England. Congratulations, perhaps, good wishes. But urgent? At such a time? Christ!

Urgent, in a blurred stencil across the top.

Jason critically ill. Please come with all possible haste. James Harrington.

That was all it said.

CHAPTER SEVEN

'Berthe, there is no time now. I can't think. I—'

The telegram shook in Anna's hand; she stared down at it, reading it over and over again without really taking it in.

'Miss Farnell, may I help in any way?'

Berthe spoke quickly, sympathetically, as she reached out her work-roughened hands to steady Anna's trembling shoulders. This was too bad. It really was too bad.

She had been a dancer once herself. She knew all about it, the tensions, the tightly-wound springs of concentration that are a dancer's body and her heart.

She sometimes thought of ballerinas as finely-bred racehorses. Both needed careful exercising, both ate a lot and had trouble with their ankles, and both had been painted by Degas.

Berthe hadn't been a ballerina—she had never really wanted that, and she hadn't been good enough for it anyway, so it was just as well. But she had been a dependable member of the Opera's *corps* from the time she was nineteen until her marriage six years later.

She had never regretted her retirement then. A year later, her figure had thickened woefully with her son's birth, and a year after that even more with her daughter's. She hadn't regretted that either.

But she loved dancing, the atmosphere of the large, dedicated Company, and she had always had a talent for sewing; her mother had seen to that. So when the children went to school Berthe went back to work, into the Opera's wardrobe department: just being back in the world she loved was grand, and they paid her.

Berthe spoke quietly. 'Miss Farnell, above all you must calm yourself. You will dance within minutes, and no matter what has happened there is no time for you to do anything about it until after the performance. Now tell me quickly what *I* must do, and I shall do my best to comply.'

Anna's confusion and weariness lifted, and she straightened her shoulders.

'Please try—try to find Lepage. Take this with you, ask him to read it, and ask him to try to arrange a flight for me from Orly to Birmingham as soon as possible. Tell him that Jason is my brother, that James Harrington is our family doctor. Tell him I have no full explanation, nothing but this telegram to show him. I'll talk with him afterwards.'

Berthe listened carefully, her brown eyes solemn in her round, motherly face.

'You are certain it is that serious? There is tomorrow evening, and the matinée on the following day, the rest of the Festi—'

'Berthe, please. Just do what I ask as quickly as you can. My brother is gravely ill. Please.'

There was no time then to do otherwise, no time for speculation or for further discussion, no time even for Anna's customary moments of blind panic.

Berthe nodded, brushed Anna's cheek with a quick, affectionate kiss, and turned to go.

Moments later Anna was Odette, emerging from the enchanted lake, shaking water from her feathers, changing from a swan into a beautiful woman, and Dominic/Siegfried was lifting her, leading her into their first *pas de deux*.

Nothing else but that. No Jason, no home, no danger, no conscious dimension of time or space other than the forest by moonlight, and Odette dancing to her Prince.

There were several interruptions in that evening's performance, several pauses while the delighted audience applauded pieces which especially pleased them: the four little swans (as Lepage had predicted), the French character dancers who so vividly created Prince Siegfried's mother and the evil Baron Von Rothbart, the Spanish dancers in Act III, Dominic as Siegfried in several scenes. Longest of all was the deafening roar of praise for Anna's breathtakingly perfect solo as Odile; the audience stood, just as the orchestra had done in rehearsal, to pay homage to her mastery of the spectacular chain of *fouettés*. If it was a circus trick, they didn't seem to care.

When the curtain rang down on the final scene the house exploded with delight. The curtain came up again and flowers rained across the footlights until they made a thick carpet along the entire width of the stage front.

Again and again and again they called for the Company with shouts of 'Bravo!' and furious applause. It was for Anna and Dominic, for all the other dancers, for Lepage; then for Dominic and for Anna once more.

They stood together in a daze, Anna's arms filled with as many flowers as they could possibly hold, her eyes misted with tears of exhaustion, and gratitude, and love.

Then she remembered James Harrington's telegram.

Dominic had changed into formal evening dress for the lavish party which would celebrate the opening night.

'Anna, you're still a swan, you silly! Come on, *chérie*. If we don't hurry there won't be any food left.'

That was usually enough to galvanize her into action no matter how tired she was after a performance. Too many London society matrons, when lionizing dancers, do not seem to feel called upon to provide any refreshment more substantial than a very light buffet and plenty of champagne. Sometimes, by the time the dancers arrive, there's nothing much left except a plate of wilting cheese straws and a few cream crackers begged from a harassed caterer's man.

'I'm not hungry,' she answered dully. 'Besides, I've got to wait for Jean. I've got to talk to him. I sent the dresser away.'

Anna buried her face in her hands, and her next words were so muffled Dominic thought he couldn't possibly have heard them correctly. 'I have to go home. Tonight, if I can.'

He came swiftly to kneel beside her, tilted her chin very gently until she was looking at him. There were tracks of recent tears through the heavy make-up, and her eyes were a mess.

'Jason is ill. There was a . . . a telegram at the end of the first act. It—I—I asked Berthe to take it to Jean, to ask him to arrange a flight for me as soon as possible.'

'What happened, *chérie*?'

She wrenched away, choking on a sob. 'I don't . . . know. It was marked "urgent", from James. He simply said that Jason is—critically ill, and that I must come home with all possible haste.'

'Oh, God be merciful!' It was a prayer.

Dominic put an arm around her shoulders and nestled her to his heart, heedless of the smudged pancake and rouge and mascara against the starched ruffles of his evening shirt.

They remained still, silently together. Then:

'Now, my dearest love, come. We must be practical. No matter what happens, you would prefer not to face it dressed as the Swan Queen, is that not so?'

The ghost of a grin flitted across her smeared face, and

she touched his hair. 'Probably not,' she said.

'Very well. So, you must shower and change while I wait here for Jean. When he comes, we shall speak to him together. We'll think of something—'

'What *can* we possibly think of? Not even the great Jean Lepage can change something like this!'

Anna flushed and bit her lip, ashamed. 'I'm sorry, love. But it must be something terribly serious or James would never have sent that message. I'll have to go home as soon as I can.'

'Yes, darling, we will both have to go—'

'No! Not you as well, Dominic. You can't.'

'Anna, we shall see what is best for us to do. But first you must get dressed.'

'Very good advice,' Jean said from the doorway. 'I have been on to every airline this side of Athens. I tried also to reach one or two friends with private planes. There is no possibility of flying from Paris to Birmingham before nine o'clock tomorrow morning. I thought of your flying to London instead, of course, but—' He glanced at his watch. 'There was no point. No trains after midnight.'

'Jean!'

'I received your message, Anna. I can say only that I am sorry. The most constructive thing I can think of for the moment is that we try to telephone your doctor, or your parents' home. You will not want to spend the entire night not knowing—'

'Oh Jean, you're kind. I had no idea—'

'That I was kind?'

'Oh, of course not that, but . . .'

'Anna, I too have a family. Nothing is more important, nothing.'

'The Festival—'

'There is always another Festival. But not so another brother, eh? If all is well, perhaps you will be able to return to finish this one. If not—bah! We shall not think in terms of "if not".

'In the meanwhile, dear Anna, life's emergencies are what understudies are for, not so? If it is any consolation at all, my spies—eavesdropping as usual during the interval—have assured me that this evening was an unparalleled *coup* for us all.'

They tried without success to ring the Farnells, James Harrington, and Elmwood Community Hospital (which Dominic belatedly thought of as a logical place to try) or anyone else in Pendleton at all.

The circuits to England were engaged, or the international operator didn't reply, or the telephone system generally was so snarled up by mechanical shortcomings that it simply wasn't possible to get through. In any case, they didn't.

They gave it up finally; there was no point in persisting all night, nor any point in Anna and Dominic returning to their hotel in the hope that James or her parents could get through by telephone to them.

The three of them went together to Madame Riccio's party, though they didn't feel very festive about it. When it turned out there was no food left at all, and very little champage, Lepage insisted on taking them out to the most cheerful all-night bistro he could think of.

He joked with them, crisis or no, anxious to see them refuelled after the evening's hard physical labour.

'Dearest Anna, you are my favourite ballerina. I beg of you, take some broth at the very least. I know you are worried, but great dancers are not noticeably improved by malnutrition, so . . . please. As for Dominic, poor thing, it is he who carted you about for several hours. Slender and lovely though you are, you are not really made of feathers. He must eat too.'

Tears

Every time Lepage excused himself (for no other real reason than to leave the two of them alone together) Anna and Dominic had the same discussion.

'You can't come with me, Dominic. It's bad enough he's losing one of us, but—'

'There you go again. Anna, we've done the première of *Swan Lake*. Now it makes little difference who dances our roles in the rest, so long as the dancers are competent. I've an understudy too, you know, and I cannot allow you to face this alone.'

'I shan't *be* alone. There will be mum and dad and James. And it *does* make a difference. You know very well that if Jean has to put poor Francesca into Odette/Odile, he'll have to modify a lot of what he's written. She wasn't able to do the twiddly bits in rehearsal, so there's no reason to think she can do them tomorrow evening, and every third evening for a month. You've got to be here to partner her, to help her.'

Francesca Montpelier was a good dancer, but she hadn't the stamina or the drive or the steely control necessary to do thirty-four consecutive *fouettés*. Few ballerinas had; that had been the point of writing them into *Swan Lake* for Anna Farnell.

'Pierre can partner her. He's good.'

'Sure he is. But Dominic, it's—it's unprofessional for both of us to leave when only one of us needs to. It's allowing our personal lives to get too much in the way, don't you see?'

At last he was made to.

When Lepage took his leave of them he was still worried. But he was exhausted too, almost as tired as they were.

He was so tired that his relief at the news that Dominic would stay with the Festival showed—very briefly—in his eyes. For once he looked his age.

'But are you sure?' he asked. 'You must not allow work to come before life, ever. Not even when work is so tightly bound with life. It merely seems so, you see, until a loved one is seriously ill.'

'I am *not* sure, Jean,' Dominic admitted. 'But Anna is determined. We have agreed that if there is need, she'll send for me.'

It was left that way. Lepage drove them to their hotel, and the two of them clung together desperately through a sleepless dawn, frightened, holding one another close for comfort, cruelly cheated of what was to have been the biggest celebration of their careers.

In the morning Lepage picked them up and drove them to Orly. When Dominic put Anna on the plane he was still holding the first reviews, which the three had shared without much real energy over a hurried breakfast.

Lepage's *Swan Lake*, they said, was the finest production of that ballet to be staged in Paris within living memory, and its principals miraculously gifted—probably the finest dancers of their generation, anywhere in the world.

CHAPTER EIGHT

Anna was startled to find James Harrington waiting for her at the airport in Birmingham. She wondered how he could have known when to expect her. But that question could wait.

'What is it? What's happened to Jason? We were so very frightened, and I came as quickly as I could. Is he—'

'Hey, calm *down* Anna,' he said, taking her case.

His grey eyes looked sunken, weary, and his tweed jacket seemed to hang from his broad shoulders as though he had shrunk within it.

'I suggest we have a cup of coffee here before we go. I think we could both use it. It's a long drive.'

'You've been up all night,' she said. They walked into the crowded snack bar.

'So have you, by the look of it.'

'Well damn it, James, that telegram! Then I couldn't get a flight out until this morning, and we couldn't reach anybody by telephone. It was awful.'

'I know, Anna. I know, and I'm sorry, so sorry. Especially for the timing. Did the première go well?'

A tremor of annoyance shook her. He was taking his own sweet time telling her what was wrong with Jason. She was tempted to tell him exactly when his message had arrived, how it might well have ruined months of solid work for a great many people, but she dismissed the thought as petty. James hadn't sent his telegram lightly, that was sure, and he couldn't possibly have known exactly when it would reach her.

'It was a huge success, thanks,' she answered, smiling. 'I've never seen so many flowers in one place in my entire life.' She paused, and plunged on. 'James, this is torture. Please, I've got to know. Has Jason been involved in an accident?'

'We think that Jason had a medical accident,' he answered. He said the words as fast as they would come—as though, that way, they would be easier to bear. 'It isn't certain, but it looks as though he reacted very badly to a combination of drugs which were used to relieve his arthritic condition.'

'But he was doing so well! After you sent him to the hospital he seemed to have a new lease of life. Don't you remember the party in June, when he was—'

'I remember.'

The boy had been getting worse, his episodes of illness seeming to chart the days of his adolescence and keep pace with it, souring it.

The new hospital had seemed a godsend; after all, James told himself, he was no specialist. But he did know that there were more drugs available to treat Jason's condition than he himself had the knowledge or the experience to prescribe safely.

James had referred Jason to Elmwood Community Hospital; he had been jubilant when the boy so visibly improved, when the only complaint he had was of the pressure to sit his exams with respectable results.

'The reaction, if it was that, was very sudden.'

'Well, what—'

'Jason has aplastic anaemia. The red corpuscles in his blood are reduced to a dangerous level, and no attempt is being made in his bone marrow to replace them.'

'Is he going to die?'

'We hope not, Anna. The specialists at Elmwood want to attempt a bone marrow transplant, which means taking healthy tissue from a suitable donor and giving it to Jason. With any luck, the donor's marrow will take hold in his body, and he'll begin to produce red blood cells of his own again.'

Anna nodded, not out of understanding but merely to encourage James to go on.

'As you're Jason's sister, your tissue type might be compatible with his, and you might therefore be a suitable donor. That's why I sent for you so urgently. There isn't much time.'

'Is it like a—a blood transfusion, or something?'

'Something like, except it's far more sophisticated. The donor is put under anaesthetic while marrow is harvested from the hip bones. That harvest is given to the patient through a vein, and great care is taken to keep him in a sterile environment until it "takes". A lot can go wrong, but if the transplant succeeds, the patient recovers. If not—'

Anna waited, her question in her eyes.

'—if not, then nothing's really been lost, at least not from the patient's point of view. If the case is severe enough to justify a transplant and it isn't successful, then the patient would have died anyway.

'There are risks, too, though admittedly slight ones, run by the donor in the procedure. He or she is presumably a healthy human being who voluntarily submits to a surgical operation under full anaesthetic just to try to help someone else. It's not a thing to be done lightly.'

Careful here. He and Chandler had argued over this one, Chandler passionately convinced it was stupid and self-defeating and unnecessary (and harmful to medical research—yes, the pompous bastard had actually used those words) to alarm the potential marrow donor.

James had argued just as passionately that the donor had every right to know what risks he or she might be running, no matter how slight they were.

'Especially when she's my patient, Mr Chandler,' James said. 'Just as Jason is.'

Chandler winced. It was one of his team who had prescribed steroids for the boy, and when they didn't work, the penicillamine. The anaemia might have been spontaneous, but there was a case for suspecting that the combination of drugs was to blame for its onset.

'Dr Harrington, I have explained to you before, and I shall explain again.' Chandler had spoken with silky, patronizing patience. 'The theoretical risks of misadventure which are run by donors in this procedure simply do not occur in practice. I have enough experience in the field, and more than enough sterile, modern equipment in this hospital, to bring Miss Farnell through the donor process quite unharmed.'

'Always assuming she's a compatible match with her brother,' James said.

'Yes of course, Dr Harrington,' Chandler conceded, sighing. 'Always assuming that.'

'What of the emotional risks? What of the guilt, the inadequacy Anna would undoubtedly feel if her donation failed to save her brother's life?'

Chandler shuffled files on his desk. 'That would, of course, be the province of my colleagues in the psychiatric field.'

Not Chandler's department.

'Anna,' James said, 'there are risks involved in any surgical operation, just as there are risks involved in crossing roads. But if you're willing to be screened as Jason's donor, and if your tissue type is compatible with his, we can discuss them then.'

Anna nodded quickly, satisfied with that.

Lord, it could be an awful responsibility to be a doctor. So quickly believed, so utterly trusted, the village *shaman*, the wise man who can do no wrong.

Hedging with Anna, avoiding the issue of risk, James

hated himself. But after all, there would be time. And much as he disliked Thomas Chandler personally, there was no reason at all to believe the man inhuman, or his medical judgment unsound. There would be time.

'What if I'm not—compatible, or whatever?'

'Then they'll start looking elsewhere for a possible donor, perhaps to a marrow bank in one of the large teaching hospitals. But a brother's or sister's donation, if it is suitable, is least likely to be rejected. Your parents and two of your cousins have already been screened. None would do.'

James paid for the coffee and they left. During the three-hour drive to Pendleton they talked lightly of ordinary things, anything to avoid the topic of Jason's illness.

'How did you know which flight I'd be on?'

James smiled. 'That was easy. Dominic sent a telegram. No, three actually. One to your parents, one to me at home, and another to me at the hospital. He wasn't taking any chances with the girl he loves.'

'No.' Anna laughed. 'It was all I could do to persuade him to stay on in Paris without me.'

James said nothing, but he glanced across at the clear, young profile and his heart contracted.

Mr Thomas Chandler, Chief Consultant Pathologist at Elmwood Centre Community Hospital, sat behind his massive oaken desk, regarding the fragile blonde who perched so gracefully on the edge of his tooled-leather consulting chair.

He had picked the heavy old-fashioned furniture for the room himself, as well as the brocaded draperies at the aluminium-framed window behind his chair.

It was all at odds with the clean modernity of the glass and brick hospital building, but when the draperies were shut it looked well enough. It was Chandler's private reminder to himself that he had left an older, more prestigious hospital to be coaxed to Elmwood Centre.

Chandler was sixty, with the experience and the necessary string of qualifications from various colleges of medicine to make his appointment perfectly in order.

He was the biggest fish the health service had been able to catch for the senior staff of its gleaming new hospital and he knew it; it would never be a teaching centre, but he was determined to make what he could of the place, to shape it into a formidable centre of medical knowledge and skill.

With genial kindliness he said to Anna, 'Thank you for coming so quickly. Your brother is very ill, very ill indeed.'

She had seen that for herself. She and her parents, ashen-faced with shock and the effort not to weep openly in front of their son, had been permitted to sit with him briefly the day Anna arrived.

Jason looked pale and wasted, with fever glittering in his eyes. And though the sleeves of his pyjama jacket covered the angry welts of the spreading bruises which James had told her were the first visible symptom of his disease, Anna knew they were there, and she ached for him.

Of the four of them that day, Jason was by far the most animated. It was almost as if he was host at a party he was obliged to give to ease his family's grief at his dying, and that he was determined to entertain his guests. He seemed almost relieved when the nursing sister came to his bed, with the kind, smiling, firm information that it was time for his visitors to leave.

Later that afternoon Anna's preliminary blood tests began; when James told her she had proved to be histo-compatible with Jason on loci HLA A and B on chromosome 6, she nodded gravely—and went back to hospital for further tests.

Chandler pursed his lips thoughtfully and opened a fat file on his desk.

'The reactivity of your lymphocytes with your brother's is sufficiently low to allow us some measure of real hope. You are a good, if not a perfect match. In plain language, Miss Farnell: if you will agree to be Jason's marrow donor I think we can safely say we'll have a fighting chance at pulling him through this.'

He shut the file with a little thwack, folded his hands on top of it, and smiled at her.

'There will be some pain and bruising afterwards, Anna,' James said. 'After all, they'll be using your hip bones like pin cushions to get from you what Jason needs. There are other dangers of things going wrong for you because of the anaesthetic—though the odds *against* anything happening are high. But you have to give it thought, before you agree to this.'

'And if I don't, and they can't find someone else in time, Jason will die.'

There was no need for James to answer that.

It crossed Anna's mind to try to reach Dominic in Paris before she gave her formal, written consent for the doctors to proceed. Almost at once she was ashamed of her hesitation. Jason was her brother, and she loved him. If she didn't try to help him and he died, how could she live, or dance, or love, or even face herself in the mirror, ever again? She signed the forms.

Dominic rang her that evening. Yes, Jason was alive, though very ill; no, she couldn't come back to Paris; yes, Dominic must stay there, to salvage what he could of Lepage's season.

The connection was bad, but between bursts of static

and interference Anna tried to explain what was wrong, and what was going to be done to try to put it right. She would undergo a simple operation, she told him; it was a matter of life and death to Jason, to receive new bone marrow to replace enough of his own to make him well again.

Dominic was concerned for Jason, but he was far more concerned for Anna. He heard the word 'operation' clearly enough; he said he would come at once.

Anna talked with him long enough to make absolutely sure he understood that there was no need for him to come rushing back to England, to her side.

CHAPTER NINE

'Anna?'

That was Carole, the young nurse who had joked with her before she fell asleep.

'Anna? Anna, darling?'

'Anna, we're with you, love.'

That was mother; she could smell the lemon verbena scent, and feel the soft, cool hand stroking her cheek, reaching gently beneath the bedclothes for her hand.

Dominic was there as well. He said 'Anna? Anna, darling?' That wasn't possible. No, Dominic was in Paris.

Anna tried to open her eyes, and just managed it; her vision swung in a hazy arc and focused briefly on the window.

She could see the rooftops and church spires of Pendleton. In the far distance she watched the bridge by the old Victorian water mill turning to silver filigree against the setting sun.

Dominic had not been standing beside mother with his arms filled with flowers. He couldn't be.

'Where—is—Jason?'

'Jason is fine, love.' *That was mother's voice.* 'He's sitting up in his bed watching *World of Sport* on television, eating his tea. Dad is with him, and it's all right, Anna. It's over now, and everything is fine.'

Jason had to stay in a special bubble which the doctors built for him. It had air filters and a port hole and special arm-and-glove fittings so that mum and dad could hold his hand sometimes.

The doctors and nurses had to dress up in space suits and crawl through the port hole to be with him while they looked after him, and everything inside the bubble had to be scrubbed and scrubbed and scrubbed again and then irradiated until it was germ-free.

'Even the food,' Jason said. 'Ugh. Ever tried a sterile egg and a piece of sterile toast? I've got to stay in here until the transplant starts to grow and they're sure there's no infection. Thank God for the television. If it wasn't for that I'd go off my nut with boredom. Apart from that, it's just like Star Trek.'

Dominic was with Jason in the Star Trek *bubble. Dominic bowed, with his arms full of flowers.*

Jason waved out at her, grinning encouragement and making a 'thumbs up' sign when she was wheeled past him into the shining, whining lift, down into the theatre beneath a canopy of speeding ceilings.

Dominic said, 'Anna? Anna, *chérie,* I'm here with you.'

She and Jason were in the germ-free isolator together, down by the canal, fishing with dad on a hot Saturday afternoon.

Dad was outside the bubble, sitting on the grassy bank in his old gardening slacks and his slouchy straw hat; Jason reached into one of the arm-and-glove fittings to be able to hold his fishing rod.

'It isn't germ-free,' Jason said.

Dominic was there, inside with Jason, with his arms full of flowers. How did they manage to scrub the flowers?

When she woke up fully it was dark. A nurse came with a small torch, squeaking across the lino like a comforting mouse. Anna told her that her hips hurt, that they were on fire, and the nurse gave her two tablets in a fluted paper cup and water in a plastic tumbler; the nurse held her hand in the dark until she went to sleep again.

'She was exhausted to begin with,' James said. 'It's understandable that her resistance was low. But the inflammation isn't very serious, Martin. The registrar seems quite confident of that, and the consultant agrees. They've given her enough antibiotic cover to knock it on the head quickly, and mild sedatives for pain.'

'I'm worried,' Martin said, 'and Helen's frantic. I don't know why all this business blew up in the first place, but it only seems to be getting worse. If anything happens to Anna, I'll—'

'Steady on, Martin,' James said. 'She'll be fine in a few days.'

Anna thought she heard that, but she wasn't sure.

She knew they had cover though.

Francesca Montpelier would cover for her. Francesca was a good dancer, though she probably wouldn't be able to do all those pirouettes without a partner to steady her. Dominic would know what to do, though, and the audiences would never realize it hadn't been planned that way all along.

She fixed her eyes on a spot just to the left of centre-stage, the plume on one of the courtiers' elaborate hats. Each time the plume came into view again, she knew she had completed one more turn. Thirty-two/thirty-three/thirty-four.

She had done it. But God, it was painful!

Someone took a photograph then, several people did. Beyond the courtier's plume she could sense rather than see the sudden pinpoint flashes of blue light beyond the brilliance of the lighted stage.

Dad took a photograph too, on the Sunday baby Jason was brought out of doors into the garden for the first time. It was a sunny day, very warm, with mum's first roses fragrant on the air; she was seven, a big sister, dressed in her best party frock and her shiny black shoes and white ankle socks.

She sat in a folding garden chair, and mum crawled through the port hole of the Star Trek *isolator bubble and placed the baby ever so carefully into her arms, and then dad said 'Smile, love!' and his camera clicked. She could smell the roses.*

Dominic placed a spray of flowers on the bed beside her.

Anna struggled to open her eyes, to focus them, and at last she managed it.

There were flowers everywhere: in vases along the window-ledge, on her night-stand, even on the bed.

'Dominic? You're in . . . Paris.'

'I was in Paris, *chérie*, and now I'm here with you.'

'What about . . . Jean, Francesca?'

'Shh, Anna, it was nearly finished. Jean insisted I come. The flowers are a little the worse for time and flying the Channel, but—' He shrugged expansively. 'I couldn't very well leave them behind, could I?'

'But—the première was weeks ago. How long have you been here?'

'Three days.'

'Three days! Where have I been all that time?'

Anna struggled to sit up, but she flinched at the hot needles of pain in her hips and lay back again, exhausted. Dominic reached out to brush a tendril of hair off her forehead, to soothe her.

'James said it would hurt a bit, but this is ridiculous,' she said. 'I'm thirsty.'

'Lie still until the nurse comes back, darling. You've been ill, feverish after the operation. But you're better now, and in a day or so they promise you'll be good as new again.'

'And . . . Jason?'

'The good news is that he's well enough to complain so bitterly about the food they're threatening to throw him out of hospital, space bubble and all. He asked me to give you this.'

Dominic handed her a crudely-drawn sketch of Mr Spock in his *Star Trek* gear, captioned by a message:

'There's not room enough in this ship for both of us. Get out, and soon!'

Anna laughed. 'This is great! Jason at his corniest.'

'Honestly, Anna, they sound very optimistic about the whole thing. Cautiously, of course, because no one will really know for sure that he's accepted the transplant until he shows a normal blood count.'

'You sound like one of the doctors.'

'Naturally. I was always a great mimic and a quick study, was I not?'

'Oh certainly, and modest with it.'

Anna had meant to ask him whose idea it was that he come rushing to her side. Suddenly, she didn't care. It was enough that Dominic was with her. She was content to be able to feel her hand in his, to laugh up into his dark eyes, able to pretend that the whole terrible nightmare was not so serious; that it would end happily, and soon.

There was one thing on her mind, one thing she had to know. Before the surgery she had been assigned a bed in a ward full of cheerful, chattering women, all cosily settled into place with their vases of flowers and their fever charts, their amazing number of stitches, their curlers, furry slippers, shared-out chocolates and Lucozade.

But Anna's was the only bed in the small blue room in which she woke up, and she wondered why she had been moved.

'Oh, because your father raised hell. I wish you could have been awake to enjoy it.'

It was inconceivable. Martin Farnell was not a hell-raiser. He was a natural-born member of a queue: deferential, soft-spoken, apologetic, self-effacing, kind; he was English.

'My *father?* With whom, Dominic, and why?'

'Oh, with all the big noises. He said very firmly that they've messed you about as much as he was prepared to stand, and that the least they could do to make it up was to provide you with privacy and every comfort possible. So here you are. Please take note of your adjoining bathroom, Madame.'

'Just like that?'

'Just like that. Unlimited visiting hours too. Naturally I was all for that.'

Dominic had been sitting on a chair beside her bed. When he stood up, Anna was afraid he was about to leave. Instead, with great care not to jar her, he leaned down and kissed her very thoroughly. She arched to meet him without thinking about it, feeling no pain at all.

CHAPTER TEN

She twisted her foot, her right foot, and it began to throb. She'd been at the end of the 'mad' scene in Giselle, *and when she fell dead, her heart broken by Count Albrecht, she twisted her foot. It was her own damned fault.*

She had danced the part so many times. She ought to know how to fall properly on stage without twisting her foot.

Anna moaned, and then began to weep with the pain; she cried out.

Elaine Warwick was the duty sister that night. She'd been a friend of Helen Farnell's since they met in Daniel Rogerson's ante-natal clinic when they were both pregnant with their first children at the same time. It grieved her as a woman and a nurse that poor Helen's two were caught up in this grim struggle for Jason's survival.

She came squeaking into the room in her soft-soled shoes, holding her torch so it wouldn't shine directly into Anna's face.

'What is it, poppet?'

'I fell. I . . . know it was clumsy of me, but I twisted my foot. I'll have to . . . massage it, and . . . soak it. Possibly I'll have to . . . wrap it. But I don't think I'll be able to dance . . . on it this evening. I'm sorry . . .'

'I'd better have a look at it, Anna,' Elaine said. 'Which foot is it?'

'Right . . .'

Elaine switched on the lamp attached to the headboard.

She adjusted it carefully, then she lifted back the blankets.

The right foot was swollen; above it, along the calf, the leg was puffy and red and hot to the touch.

'I think it's best if doctor looks at this, love,' Elaine said. She spoke with as much professional unconcern as she could muster.

There was a blood clot in the child's vein; you couldn't miss a thing like that, not if you'd been nursing for nearly thirty years.

Deftly she raised Anna's head and extracted one of her pillows; she placed it at the foot of the bed, and lifted Anna's leg so it was resting on it, slightly elevated. Anna moaned again, and then she was awake; she could see the soft, boneless protruberance at the end of the bed that was her swollen foot.

'What's wrong with it?' she whispered, frightened.

Elaine patted her hand, and forced a reassuring smile. 'We'll see what the doctor says, love. He'll come straight away.'

Elaine squeaked out again. When she reached the dimly-lighted corridor and was out of Anna's view she broke into a little run.

Rob Morgan was the registrar on call. He was asleep in the austere cubicle provided for that purpose when the summons came. He came alert at once, glanced at his watch, noted with no little satisfaction that he was able to climb into his trousers, tie his shoes and knot his tie, comb his hair, and shrug into his white coat in forty seconds flat. He'd gone to sleep in his shirt and underwear and socks, of course; all the night-duty registrars did that.

Permanently exhausted by frequently broken sleep and infrequent intervals of time to call his own, Rob was destined to become a good surgeon, perhaps a great one—if only because the obvious, traditional burdens of his profession seldom occurred to him as such.

He had wanted to help people, to make them better, since he was a child; that pure, simple impulse had survived his training. He still wanted to help people, and he knew what he was doing most of the time. When he didn't, he had the humility and grace to admit it to himself, and sometimes even to a patient, and he had the sense to ask for help.

Rob's chief personal joy in life was to write long, rambling letters explaining all this to his girlfriend in London, though when he thought of her he always amended 'girlfriend' to 'fiancée' with proud, slightly wistful optimism.

They couldn't meet often, but she wrote back to him: tender, amused, sketchy little notes about his hard-working life as a doctor, and about her life as a drama student. That was enough for the moment because it had to be.

Her name was Janet, though she styled herself Tania and insisted that Rob call her that. When he was able to be with her in London, a slightly self-conscious overnight visitor in her flat in North Kensington, she dragged him out to every cultural or pseudo-cultural or just plain fun event she could think of from jazz concerts at the Lyric in Hammersmith to pre-dawn antique markets in the streets of Bermondsey. She cheerfully ignored his half-hearted protests that he really ought to study instead.

They would make a good marriage, if they got that far. Tania loved Rob, and cared for him, and she would provide the grace note of fantasy to his grimly realistic, dedicated life.

She would teach their children to make butterflies out of Origami paper, and to love poetry.

She would coax him into relaxation too, into the suspended responsibility of sheer make-believe, like the time he'd been down to see her and she'd taken him to the ballet. It was *Giselle*, he remembered. Wonderful.

A coincidence niggled. The ballet, the ballet, the ballet...

Rob had seen 'Farnell, Jason', and 'Farnell, Anna', on his list when he came on duty.

'Farnell, Jason' was Chandler's big bid to be a hero by pulling off a successful bone marrow transplant, thereby cocking a snook at the major centres where it was done routinely every day of the week. No, it wasn't quite fair to think of it that way.

Chandler knew what he was doing. He had the equipment and the laboratories for it too, and all the necessary drugs. He even had a matching donor, the boy's sister. And Jason Farnell was a pretty sick boy.

Besides, Chandler had been indirectly responsible for the kid's condition. Or so it was rumoured around the hospital, Rob amended carefully. Though he couldn't imagine how. Chandler might be pompous and arrogant and ambitious, but he was certainly a fine doctor, well-respected if not liked.

Unless some cowboy on Chandler's staff had prescribed Pharmaceutical Allsorts in an attempt to treat some other condition Jason Farnell had. Rob didn't know; he couldn't judge.

A doctor's first important lesson: Thou Shalt Not Be Responsible for Everybody, and Thou Shalt Not Judge Thy Colleagues. But it bothered him, and he wondered.

Rob had heard someone say that Anna Farnell was a dancer. Oh, but she couldn't be the same one. There were lots of dancers, weren't there? You certainly wouldn't find the Anna Farnell of Covent Garden's

Giselle languishing in a backwater like Elmwood Centre.

Sweet Christ, not with a suspected thrombosis in her right leg!

Rob Morgan was on Elaine Warwick's ward within six minutes of her call. Even before he entered Anna's room he saw that she was the same young woman who had given him two hours of the most astonishing, unexpected pleasure of his life.

The same expressive eyes and mouth, the same fine, fragile bone structure, the same . . . presence, Tania would have called it.

Rob caught his breath, and pretended to fumble with his notes in the doorway, shy. But Elaine Warwick was right behind him, so finally Rob walked to the bed and Anna smiled up at him.

'I'm sorry, doctor. I must have disturbed your rest, and you must be tired.'

He smiled back at her and told her he didn't mind, but his eyes were serious as he probed the tenderness along her leg. The vein was hard, blocked.

Anna shut her eyes against the pain. 'What's wrong with it, doctor?'

He straightened and exchanged a glance with Elaine over Anna's head.

'A blood clot has formed in one of the veins in your leg,' he said. 'I'm going to give you a shot of heparin—that's an anticoagulant—and something to ease the pain. Tomorrow I'll send your own doctor to have a look at it. It's quite common after surgery, really; not usually anything much to worry about. You'll be on your feet within a week or so.'

That much was true. He didn't add that she would be sent home still taking anticoagulants by mouth, that she would have to continue taking them for months, coming back to hospital regularly for blood tests and physiotherapy, as an outpatient.

Nor did he tell her that in something like a quarter of the cases, thrombophlebitis patients were left with permanent muscular weakness, swelling or aching in the affected leg.

If she were one of the unlucky ones, she would never be able to dance professionally again.

CHAPTER ELEVEN

It was raining the day Anna left hospital, a steady, mournful, relentless downpour which promised never to stop, denying the very existence of the sun.

Pendleton itself was built on a hill, a toy town of red brick interspersed with trees, tidy and visibly brave beneath the sullen sky. But the rest of Elmwood Centre was disposed along the shallow valley below it, and Martin had to drive past several of the new estates to get them home.

There were houses grouped in rows of ninety at a stretch, bleak, grey, hopeless-looking structures of corrugated aluminium, squatting in raw brown mud like so many trains shunted into sidings.

Now and again there was evidence of life: a woman with a pram, shivering in a bus shelter; a couple of school kids running in bright yellow macs; a bicycle forgotten in somebody's barren garden. They all seemed out of place, human beings and human artifacts on the white, cold, uncaring surface of the moon.

Anna sat with Dominic in the back seat, staring out at the rainscape without really seeing it, thinking her own thoughts, huddled in the protection of her warm plaid jacket, holding Dominic's hand.

Once or twice Helen glanced back over her shoulder to smile at them, but no one spoke.

Helen had brought a pair of Anna's oldest jeans for her to wear going home. They were flared at the bottoms, unfashionably so, but they disguised her swollen leg. The ancient pair of moccasins she brought accommodated Anna's still-puffy right foot.

'It's not forever, you know,' Chandler told them in his office before Anna was released. 'With time and care and exercise—*and* patience,' he added, wagging his index finger playfully in Anna's direction, 'this should clear itself up beautifully. Don't forget to take the anticoagulants, and to come back for tests and physiotherapy.'

'How long will it take to clear itself up?' Martin asked abruptly.

Anna stared at him. She had never in her life heard her father use such a brusque tone to anyone.

'That very much depends on factors no one can predict with accuracy, Mr Farnell,' Chandler answered, unperturbed.

He busied himself with some papers on his desk, an unsubtle hint that the interview was finished.

It was not, quite.

'I'm very tired of hearing that phrase,' Martin said clearly. 'It's the only one you doctors seem to use in connection with this case, no—these cases—of my son and daughter. As things are, you can't or won't tell us how long Jason will be in that—thing—you've got him in, or even if he'll ever come out of it alive. Now you're avoiding the issue of my daughter's leg and foot—'

'Mr Farnell—'

'If we were in the United States, Mr Chandler, I would give serious consideration to attempting a lawsuit, and a consequent investigation into why all this was necessary in the first place.'

Chandler blanched, but Martin ignored that. 'As we are not, the best we can hope for is that both my children will come out of this incredible medical tangle in good health.'

'I suppose it's debatable whether my daughter's career is as important as yours, Mr Chandler, but it *is* her career, and it's important to her and to us and a great many members of the public. Now, how long will it be before she'll be able to dance again?'

Martin spoke calmly, doggedly persistent, while Helen looked worriedly from him to the doctor and back again as though she wished she could do something to stop what sounded to her like a fight.

Anna sat quite still, watching her father, and Dominic stood behind her with his hands resting on her shoulders.

'I can understand your concern, Mr Farnell, but—'

'But nothing, Mr Chandler. I asked you a direct question.'

'But there is no direct answer,' Chandler said. 'There seldom is in these cases. Anna will need to take anticoagulant drugs for at least three months. As for her resumption of her dancing—' He shook his head wearily. 'We simply have to do our best and . . . hope for the best.'

'What happens if it comes to the worst?' Anna asked.

The two men had been discussing her future literally over her head, as if she wasn't there. Chandler looked at her and smiled, and his tone softened.

'Anna, it really is best not to think in negative terms. If you take the medication, and exercise your leg carefully and faithfully, there is no reason to think you won't recover fully, really not.'

It was left there, the interview concluded on a note of restrained civility all round, though Martin was far from satisfied by Chandler's vague attempts at reassurance.

Remembering it later, he flushed again with anger; Chandler had said nothing about Jason, or how long he would be confined to his sterile plastic prison before the doctors pronounced him well enough to leave it, and to live.

James Harrington did his best, but he wasn't much

help either. Not that he didn't try. He was the Farnells' friend as well as their doctor, and for the first time in the friendship there was a element of tension.

It was hard for James to say, after a meal which they had shared, which was meant to relax them all:

'I don't know, Martin. Honestly, I don't know what's going to happen with Jason—or even with Anna, for that matter. If I did, I'd tell you. We're all waiting, and hoping. Doctors are just people, Martin. You've got to try to remember that.'

A week passed, and Dominic was still in Pendleton with Anna. When she reminded him that he really should go back to London and the Company, he brushed it off lightly, unconcerned.

He couldn't bear to leave her, and there was no immediate reason why he should. Lepage had paid them both the full salaries they had agreed for the entire Festival, and when Dominic finally did go down to London for the day, to check the flat and to speak to Steven Harwood, Steven offered him compassionate leave without even being asked.

'For as long as it takes Anna to get well,' Steven said. 'I'm keeping you both on salary for the duration. I've written to her, telling her not to worry about anything at all.'

So Dominic went back to King's Cross, and from there to Elmwood Centre and to Pendleton, and a week passed into two.

In some ways life assumed the quality of an extended holiday.

The two of them played Mastermind and snakes-and-ladders and Monopoly on the sitting-room floor, or they watched television; sometimes Dominic insisted Helen put her feet up while he did the cooking.

In other ways, of course, the atmosphere was so badly fraught with anxiety it seemed that nothing would ever be normal again.

Anna had never been ill in her life except for the minor ailments of childhood. Her frustration with her leg amounted to desperation, and there were times, alone with Dominic, when she behaved like an exuberantly healthy animal which has been suddenly, inexplicably, and cruelly injured.

The pain in her hips had subsided completely, and within a fortnight of leaving hospital her foot returned more or less to its normal size. But her calf was still distended, the vein hard and sore to the touch.

'It's ugly! So ugly I can't bear to look at it.'

'Anna, if your poor leg is swollen and sore for a while, then you must love it more than ever.'

Her lips tightened. 'Kiss it better, I suppose.'

'Something like that. You must be patient.'

'Patient! What if it never gets any better than this? What then?'

'Darling, you mustn't think that way.'

'What if I can't dance on it, ever again?'

'That would be very, very sad, Anna, but it wouldn't change my love for you.'

'But I'm your partner too, Dominic. Or I was. Don't you remember?'

There was nothing he could say to that, nothing he could do except to help her through the exercises with religious care, to curtail their formerly rambling walks through the countryside because of her easy fatigue, to remind her over and over again that he loved her, to try every way he could think of to persuade her to love herself again.

None of that was easy for either of them, but it would have been far worse if they hadn't enjoyed complete and respected privacy within the Farnells' home.

Helen and Martin had known about their relationship almost from its beginning. Anna and Dominic slept together, made love together, 'like a married couple', Helen said to herself, accepting it. The acceptance was due not so much to broad-minded enlightenment as common sense. It was so, a fact, so why should she and Martin pretend it wasn't, or try to inflict pressure to have it otherwise?

Anna was their daughter, but she was no longer a child; besides, they were fond of Dominic, and they respected both of them. That Martin and Helen were themselves happy together had a lot to do with it.

The single bed of Anna's childhood had long since been replaced by a double one, without comment, and from the time Anna first brought Dominic to her parents' home she shared her room with him whenever they stayed there.

In those weeks their loving commitment served them well, though there was a problem even there.

Anna had been on the Pill before the thrombosis in her leg which made the Pill dangerous for her to take. She was self-conscious at first about the clumsy apparatus of mechanical birth control. Dominic managed to make her see the humour in the situation by suggesting they go together to the only chemist in Pendleton to request (in loud, carrying voices) a gross of French letters.

'In shocking pink,' he specified.

'You're wicked.'

'I want you.'

'Even with this leg?'

'Oh Anna, Anna, with blue teeth and orange hair, or even with a hairy wart on your chin, you'd still be you.'

'You're seducing me . . .'

'Ah well, if you call this seduction, I'll have you know I can do a whole lot better . . .'

Behind their firmly closed door, Anna and Dominic could forget everything but the tenderness and fire that swept them together in the night.

Martin was out all day, chief accountant for a local builders' merchant; they were doing a booming trade, he said.

'The new town's the best thing that ever happened to the firm. Some of these houses fall apart quicker than the Corporation can repair them, and they come to us for materials. "Slap it up and fix it later," that's their motto.'

Martin worked all day and Helen kept house, her daily routine lengthened by the need to do for Dominic and Anna as well as for Martin and herself. In the daytime, Jason would have been at school if he hadn't been in hospital.

But Jason was in hospital. When Martin came home in the evenings he and Helen, Anna and Dominic were all together, and Jason was not with them at the dinner table.

After dinner they went to visit him, smiling together, Anna trying hard not to limp, Helen trying equally hard not to weep, Martin trying not to look worried, Dominic trying to think of some new joke to cheer them all.

James Harrington joined them once or twice for dinner, and went with them to hospital; almost always, if he didn't do that, he would be there when they arrived, or he would come in to see Jason while they were there.

James had gradually replaced the abrasive Chandler and the other consultants as the Farnells' major source of information about Jason's progress; he did his best to keep them fully informed without sounding like a medical textbook or frightening them with the minutest details of Jason's daily regime.

He described the injections which were given to prevent rejection of the graft, the regular transfusions of blood products which would be given until it 'took', the carefully strict nursing routine which protected the boy from infection. Mentioning matters almost casually, to demystify them as much as he could, he did his best to make it all sound like the cocoon of expert care around Jason that it actually was.

It was becoming steadily and heartbreakingly more difficult for Martin and Helen to understand why their son had to remain in his isolator. He was out of bed and sitting in a chair within its confines more often than not when his family saw him, and he looked—and said he felt—stronger than he had for months.

His arthritis had recurred, though Jason never mentioned that to his parents or his sister. James knew it, but he didn't mention it either. He would cross that bridge when they came to it, when they were sure Jason was going to make it.

Jason said, three weeks to the day after the transplant, that he thought he could actually feel it growing. He was restless, anxious to be up and about; he missed school, and he was always hungry. His most recent blood tests indicated that he might indeed be right.

That was the evening he and Dominic conducted a long, hilarious dialogue on the telephone which connected the isolator with the outside world, about the exact dimensions and required topping of the pizza Jason wanted. Helen giggled and even Martin laughed aloud.

It was also the evening Martin made his halting peace with James.

'You know I don't feel any of this has been your fault,' he said as they walked into the hospital corridor together. 'I can only say I'm sorry for flying off the handle at you, and more than once. You've done a lot more than

Tears

your share for us, you always have done. I think it's about time I said that.'

'With both your children caught up in this nightmare I think you've shown remarkable restraint,' James said.

Martin grunted. 'Come back with us for coffee?'

'Not tonight, thanks. Three mums-to-be in maternity and a heart patient to be double-checked. I think I'd better stick around her awhile. But thanks, Martin.'

That night, the first in weeks, Martin slept soundly almost as soon as his head touched his pillow. Anna slept well too, in Dominic's arms. No matter what might happen to her, she had helped her brother; she was at peace.

When the telephone rang at two a.m. Helen woke, fumbled for her slippers and her dressing gown, switched on the light in the hallway outside their bedroom so as not to disturb Martin, and went downstairs to answer it.

It was James. 'You and Martin had better come to hospital as soon as you can, Helen,' he said. 'Jason is very ill.'

Helen was given a space suit and allowed to enter the isolator as soon as they arrived at hospital.

One by one, similarly outfitted and with filtered air blowing at full pressure to guard Jason, Martin and Anna and Dominic were permitted to join her briefly by turns.

When the rotation was complete, Martin went inside again and Anna and Dominic watched helplessly with James as the tableau unfolded like a storm within a crystal paperweight. Space-age mother and father with their son, with two nurses and several doctors constantly in attendance, trying to save his life against the odds.

Jason died just as the sun came up.

The cause of death was graft-versus-host-disease, in which the donor's marrow literally attacks that of the recipient, trying to destroy it.

It occurs in at least half of marrow transplant patients; twenty per cent of the time it is life-threatening, and it killed Jason Farnell.

The drug methotrexate had been given from the beginning to prevent it, and when it happened anyway they gave Jason anti-lymphocyte serum in an attempt to treat it. None of it worked.

Chandler was visibly shaken. 'Dr Harrington,' he said, 'I know you have an admirable loyalty to the truth, to keeping your patients as fully informed as possible. But I'll plead with you not to be any more specific about the actual cause of Jason Farnell's death than you must be.

'The match was good, but as you know it wasn't perfect. It seldom is. If Anna is told that her donation actually destroyed her brother's bone marrow—and that's what it would sound like to her—well, surely it would be too much for her to absorb, in her mental and physical state . . .'

For once James agreed with Chandler; for once he could see the man behind the mask of Great Doctor and admit to himself that Chandler's motives were true, his instincts perfectly correct.

James told the Farnells that Jason's body had rejected the graft. It wasn't the whole truth, but it was true enough in the sense that Jason was dead and it hadn't been anybody's fault, least of all Anna's.

Jason's funeral was simple, bare and plain to match the cold austere October.

The Farnells were vaguely Church of England. The

vicar was young and sympathetic, sober at his first time burying a boy who hadn't had a chance to grow to manhood.

The service and the interment were on a rainy Tuesday; the flowers on the grave were wet. The entire Farnell family had come, of course, as well as Helen's brother and his wife.

Jason's form master came, as did several of his classmates; they went up to Helen or to Martin and said with awkward, parent-coached courtesy: 'I offer you my deepest sympathy.'

One lad said 'symphony' by mistake, and Anna stifled an hysterical giggle, leaning on Dominic's arm.

Martin said, looking down into his son's grave:

'The boy never got his pizza, Helen, the one he wanted.'

Helen, her eyes red-rimmed and puffy, wept again.

That evening, after a dinner Martin's sister cooked, a dinner none of them wanted or really tasted, Anna helped her mother into bed, gently insisting that she take two of the tablets James prescribed to help her sleep.

Dominic took Martin to the pub. 'If I can get him drunk enough, perhaps he'll be able to cry. He needs to. Will you come with us, Anna?'

'No, but—thanks. I think I'd just like to be on my own for a bit. I'll be all right.'

Later, when Helen slept, Anna went to her room. At the *barre* Martin had installed with proud care as a surprise for her when she was ten, Anna attempted for the first time in over a month to do her warming-up exercises.

She knew she was badly out of practice; she was prepared to take it slowly, carefully.

But when her right leg throbbed with pain even as she stretched upward from the first *plié*, and she could feel it was hopeless to go on, she collapsed on the floor in despair.

Anna wept then, for her brother, for herself.

She knew then it had all been for nothing.

She knew, without logic or conscious thought, that her recovery would be slow, very slow. She knew with certainty, deeper in her heart than grief, that she would never dance beside Dominic again.

CHAPTER TWELVE

'Tell me the truth, James. It's no good my not knowing.'

Anna sat upright on the examining table and swung her legs over the side. At first glance her right leg looked perfectly normal.

She knew it wasn't, and so did he.

James had just finished examining it. The blockage of the blood clot persisted along the vein; he could feel it as a hard line along her calf.

'Every time I try to work at the *barre*—'

'Anna, you were warned to take things slowly.'

'Slowly? I haven't much choice in the matter! I can't even get past the first *plié* of a simple, elementary warm-up.'

'But that's hard work. You can't expect miracles.'

'*Not* miracles. Just to be able to do what I've been doing most of my life. This happened two months ago, nearly three, and I'm beginning to suspect—' she pointed to her leg '—that this is as far as I'm likely to get. It's no good my going on hoping if there is none.'

He sighed. 'Anna, there's always hope.'

She stared up at him angrily. 'Even Chandler said the thing should clear itself within three to four weeks. But it's been months now, and it hasn't. I don't think it's going to.'

'You're still taking the anticoagulant?'

'Every day. And still doing the prescribed exercises, and Dominic's still trying to reassure me it's only temporary, a little inconvenience.'

'Your parents?'

'We never discuss it. It's—hard enough, their losing Jason like that, without . . . this. It isn't going to go away, is it James?'

'Anna, I can't say. I don't *know*. We can only hope that it will. Even if it doesn't you'll feel improvement as time passes—'

'If enough time passes, we'll all be dead! I want to know how long it's going to be before I can go back to the Company, or if I'm even likely to be able to go back at all. Ever.'

'Anna—'

Another hard part about being a doctor was knowing where to strike a balance between the full and sometimes painful truth and a comfortable half-truth, or even a downright lie.

'Anna, your leg will improve, I'm sure of that. You'll be able to walk with greater ease, and most of the aching will go. Your blood clotting time is good, and it will probably be back to normal before long. As for your dancing . . .'

'Say it.'

'Anna, I—'

'Say it, James!'

'Anna, I'm not sure—'

'That I'll be able to go back to it,' she finished flatly.

'No, Anna. Probably not.'

'Why have you waited so long to tell me?' she whispered, anguished.

'At first no one could have predicted it, one way or the other. And news like that, a prognosis like that, coming directly on the heels of Jason's death . . . wouldn't have been tolerable. I couldn't risk piling one tragedy directly on top of another one. And I felt I had to wait until . . . you knew it anyway.'

'How long have you known?'

He ran a hand through his hair.

'Three . . . four weeks. When the vein didn't clear itself as quickly as we'd hoped. Now, even if it's cleared surgically, your leg will be in a . . . weakened state, more or less . . . permanently.'

'Do you think Dominic knows?'

'I have . . . talked with him about the possibility—'

'Behind my back.'

'Try not to feel that way about it, Anna, please. It's hard for him as well.'

'Oh yes! Pretending all this time we had a future together out of—pity!'

She spat the word angrily, remembering Dominic's unflagging gaiety, his relentlessly cheerful remarks about how wonderful it would be when she was well again, when they were back in London with the Company.

'Anna, you and Dominic *do* have a future together. He loves you, not just as a partner but as a woman. Surely you don't doubt that.'

'Working together was part of it. Always, don't you see? We were a team. Without that there won't be any point. I'd only be in his way. Dancing is his life . . . my life. As things are, he hasn't danced a step since all this happened.'

Anna's voice quavered and broke; the tears flowed unchecked down her cheeks. James fumbled for a tissue on the instruments trolley and handed it to her.

She thought she had prepared herself for the awful pronouncement about her leg; she had half-suspected it for weeks. She had expected to be able to take it courageously, or at least with dignity. But actually hearing it, even in James' careful, tactful words—the fact of discussing it out loud—was too much to bear. She felt as if she were drowning in tears and misery. She hung her head so that a shimmering length of her blonde hair half hid her face as she struggled to bring her sobs under control, to stop her whole body trembling.

'Dominic loves you, Anna. Go home, talk with him. You'll work things out together, you'll see.'

'But . . . dancing is—*was*—my life. It's all I know, and it's the same for him. It would be criminal to hold him back . . .'

'You needn't, Anna. Instead of being with him on stage, you can be waiting for him in the wings, his inspiration.'

'Hanging on for dear life to a man who feels sorry for me!'

No, never that. It would be far better to send Dominic away, to make a clean, clear break forever . . . than to sit back and watch the slow death of their love, the spectre of Dominic's sense of honour, of duty, fighting against his need to soar, to be free of a millstone.

'You needn't hang on to him, Anna,' James said firmly. 'There are dozens of things you might do. You could work in dance notation, or teach. Who knows? You might find you've a talent for choreography.'

Anna stared at him, wondering where on earth James had learned so much about the non-performing aspects of dance. Then she realized dully that Dominic must have told him something of it when they talked.

Anything to give her hope, they would have decided; anything to buoy her up, help her out of her depression. Her brother was dead, and she a partial cripple. It was best to find some way to console her, some way to keep her away from total despair.

James had kept Daniel Rogerson's cottage in the High Street. He lived there, and two afternoons each week he held surgery there for the convenience of his Pendleton patients, the old-timers, as he still thought of them.

It wasn't far from the Farnells', a quarter mile or perhaps even less. Anna walked home that day, trying to think, a pretty girl with long blonde hair bouncing on her shoulders, with only the faintest trace of a limp to indicate she had a care in the world.

She passed the draper's and the greengrocer's, and the newsagent's where Martin had bought his daily paper since before she was born, where she had spent her pocket money on sweets before she was tall enough to reach the counter: all the landmarks of her childhood, safe and familiar, her home town.

Anna saw it through the distortion of pain; it brought no comfort to her. She felt she had lost everything worth having. She would never feel at home anywhere ever again.

When she got to the Co-op she caught sight of her reflection in the glass window. Even in the heavy plaid jacket she looked slim. Thin, she thought; she had lost weight in the difficult months since—since the accident. She couldn't see her face at all clearly, but she thought it looked drawn, haggard.

She felt older. Older because the shadow of grief had touched her. She could never ever forget Jason or the tragic circumstances of his death.

Once in a while, setting the table for dinner, Anna had to stop herself from setting a place for Jason. None of them had begun to recover from his death. They might go along almost normally for days, and then something—a phrase he had used, or a book he'd been fond of—would trigger the agony again, propelling them into a fresh awareness of their loss.

It was Helen, her usually soft mouth set in grim, determined lines, who set about sorting out Jason's things.

'I want no nonsense about leaving his room the way he left it,' she said. 'That would be foolish and unhealthy. There's plenty of lads can use his clothes, and what we do decide to keep I'll pack away.'

She did all that, folding his belongings into neat parcels: this for Oxfam, that for a jumble sale, another for the attic.

Anna did her best to help, while Dominic fetched and carried boxes, and carted them off to the places Helen assigned for them. Whenever it got to be too much for her and she broke down completely, he consoled her, hugging her, stroking her hair, letting her cry.

Martin wept openly once more, just as they were about to sit down to dinner on the day after the funeral. His hoarse, jagged sobbing was terrible to hear; it was more painful to hear his embarrassed apology for it afterwards, and to be unable to comfort him for fear of making him feel worse.

After that the only visible sign of Martin's grief was that he would suddenly go even quieter than usual; his eyes would unfocus as he stared off for a moment into the middle distance.

Dominic was a comfort to each one of them, sustaining them through the worst, early weeks following Jason's death.

To Anna, mourning her brother and not at all sure what her own fate would be, Dominic was a rock of strength. She leaned on him, grateful for his presence beside her, willing herself not to think of the career he was neglecting for her sake.

She shut her eyes to everything except her love for him and his constant assurances that he loved her, and would go on loving her forever.

'But now I know the truth. You must go back to London without me, Dominic.'

'No.'

'Yes! Christmas is barely six weeks away, and Steven will need—'

'Steven and I have already discussed it, Anna.'

'You've been discussing a lot lately, haven't you? With James, with Steven. A frank discussion between you and me is overdue, wouldn't you agree?'

Anna was trembling; she had come back from James' surgery and gone directly to her room with Dominic. They were sitting on the bed, and Anna was picking invisible threads from the coverlet, avoiding his eyes.

'After Christmas we'll both go back to London, *chérie*. But for now we've got to stay here. Your parents—'

'My parents are grieving, Dominic. I know that, and that Christmas will be hard on all of us this year. That mustn't stop you getting on with your life.' Her voice was nearly a whisper; the words were stilted, almost formal. She had to force herself to say them.

'Anna, I *love* you. I love you with all my heart. I'll never stop loving you. Please, you must understand that. Nothing has changed between us.'

'Yes, it has. James admitted it this afternoon. It's unlikely I'll ever be able to—dance again.'

He took her hands in his, stopping her fingers' restless search over the coverlet.

'Look at me, Anna. Please.'

She looked up, her eyes wide, frightened pools in her white face.

'Well?'

'Darling, if that's what is to be, it's infinitely sad. I feel it too—'

'Not the way I do! It's my life, Dominic, my whole life. Years and years of it, and the whole stupid, ghastly business was such a waste. I couldn't even help Jason. Now I'm being cosseted, lied to—'

'No, Anna!'

Her eyes blazed with pain. 'Yes! Lied to. To keep my spirits up. I can't stand it.'

'Good God, Anna, how can I make you understand? You belong with me, I belong with you. Nothing can change that. Ever.'

'Belong? How?'

'Oh Anna, do let's stop this stupid quarrel. Please. What kind of life would I have without you? I love you. I *love* you, dancing or not. And you care for me . . . don't you?' He touched her face, traced her mouth.

She looked into his dark eyes, his handsome, familiar, cherished face; her vision misted with the tears that wet her lashes and threatened to spill. He took her into his arms and held her very close. She relaxed against him, allowing herself to love him, and her tears dissolved.

Later Dominic went out to buy flowers; chrysanthemums for Helen because she loved them, and for Anna, a single, perfect rose. She cradled the fragrant, blood-red bud against her cheek, her eyes dancing.

'What's this for?'

'Does there have to be a reason? Very well then, because it is not your birthday.'

They had always had that custom, Dominic's 'un-birthday' roses; he had even bought her an elegantly fragile crystal bud vase in which to put them.

For a time, everything was good again. Anna shut her eyes to the future. Dominic loved her, she loved him. Did it really matter if she couldn't dance?

They started to make plans.

'We'll keep the flat,' he said, 'and if you decide to teach, we'll find a studio. Very posh address of course—somewhere in Kensington, I should think. Cash in on all the super-mums jostling to have their little darlings coached by the best in the business.'

'Formerly the best.'

'Anna,' He sighed. 'We are not building castles in the air with gloom, all right? Rule number one: "No gloom." There is no rule number two.'

She laughed at that and shut her eyes again very tightly; she could see herself working again, and teaching began to appeal to her. Dominic would continue to dance, of course, and she would go and watch him and when he came home to her she would be there waiting.

'You will be bursting with the news of the newest apprentice Pavlova you have found in the day's class.'

'Oh, but they'll all be budding Pavlovas, Dominic!'

She would probably have to learn to cook, she thought; even that began to seem like fun. Dominic and Helen between them would create an Anglo-French culinary genius of her!

Eventually she might even manage to strengthen her leg to the point where—no, it was better not to think along those lines, better not to reach for the stars.

One afternoon she went quietly to the library to look up 'blood clots' in the reference section. She searched patiently until she found an enormous, forbidding medical dictionary, and when she had read the entry under 'Veins, diseases of,' half a dozen times, she felt she understood what had happened to her, and what she could expect.

It was best to enjoy what she could have, what she and Dominic would build together.

'Who can tell? I might even persuade you to marry me, in a fit of madness. We would then be all legalized, and maybe we should think of producing a child. Or even two!'

Anna smiled softly at that. Her life had changed, had been curtailed, limited. But only in one direction, after all. She was alive, in love. There was still a future for them, a future full of tantalizing possibilities.

They discussed it endlessly. They would work for it

together, and it would unfold for them. Above all, they would be together.

Dominic's own career was something he wouldn't discuss. He would dance. That was his profession. But he dismissed that part of the future as if it would look after itself. His prospects for international fame were assured, unaltered, money in the bank.

Anna knew that he did it deliberately to save her feelings, not to dwell on the joy she herself had known from performing. She was reminded often enough of what she had lost, and for nothing.

She sensed his delicacy and was grateful for it, though she did ask him once, hesitantly, what productions Steven had planned for Christmas, what roles Dominic had refused by postponing his return to the Company.

'Nothing very exciting,' he said. 'The usual *Nutcracker*, I suppose, and two or three others. I can't remember what they are.'

He changed the subject; they talked of the proper height of a *barre* and the age range of the children she would teach, the difficulties they might encounter in finding a good pianist for her studio, and a qualified careful tuner for the piano itself—the kind of details that breathed life into the dream and made it seem real.

The days passed for them that way. Slowly, lovingly, Dominic tried to drag Anna back from despair. And Anna tried hard to react to what Dominic was trying so hard to do for her, for both of them.

She tried to imagine herself in the new world he created with his enthusiastic, encouraging words.

But always in quiet moments her thoughts came back to the numbing truth: she could no longer dance beside him. As time passed, this was never absent from Anna's mind, blotting out everything else. She began to see Dominic's plans for their new life for what they really were, had always been: castles in the air.

Tears

She began to spend hours on her own, rehearsing little speeches which she never quite perfected, which she discarded even as she shaped them.

The words were always the same:

You must leave me. You must go back, Dominic. I can't go with you and your leaving will be unbearably painful. Go! Dance, though I can't be beside you. Go...

She couldn't bear to *say* the words, but slowly she began to feel them; she began to try to cut him free.

Dominic waited patiently, loving her, bewildered, hoping she would find her way out of her maze of pain, and back to him.

He said to her, 'Anna, talk to me. Tell me why you seem so . . . distant. Please, my love. Oh I know how you must feel, my darling! But please, please let me help you. We are together, we have life, we have love . . .'

But Anna was remembering what Régine Barrère had said to them before they left Paris, after their gruelling apprenticeship under her strict, uncompromising tutelage: '. . . together you may well build a partnership to . . . dazzle the world.'

They had nearly done it, she and Dominic, Farnell and Lautrec. Now it was finished, gone forever. Her lips moved soundlessly as she stiffened in his arms, but she said nothing. Nor did she respond to his kiss.

In the night, when Dominic reached out for her, she began to turn away, saying, 'I'm tired.'

Once when it happened Dominic awoke just before dawn, aware that Anna was sobbing quietly into her pillow. When he tried to take her into his arms she shrank away as though he was a stranger, an intruder in some terrible dream.

CHAPTER THIRTEEN

Then she saw it.

She was lingering over coffee, glancing through her father's newspaper after he left for work, wondering idly what to wear for a morning to be divided almost evenly between blood tests and physiotherapy at Elmwood Hospital

Anna hated the prospect of both, but especially the therapy and the overkill of cheer the therapist brought to her task, as if Anna was a delicate bloom who had never moved her right leg willingly in her life.

Her name was Roberta. In her green serge uniform and red elastic belt she reminded Anna of a slightly hysterical Father Christmas. Roberta wore sturdy, no-nonsense shoes, and her nose was shiny with her contempt for make-up.

'Like Rudolph the Red-Nosed Reindeer,' she described the woman to Dominic.

'I thought you said Father Christmas.' He smiled at her and ruffled her hair.

'Oh well, a bit of both. Too hearty by half.'

Going to that hospital was bad enough; Jason had died there. Sitting in the uncompromising sterility of the gleaming pathology laboratory while white-coated technicians bustled about with syringes full of her blood seemed to Anna like being processed; she felt like a fish finger.

Roberta, however, was the living limit. Roberta should have gone into the Army, Anna said. Dominic thought that was so funny he came along to see for himself, and he agreed.

Roberta smiled all the time; she was a young woman, but she boomed with all the confident authority of a sergeant-major on parade as she issued her instructions.

'*Move* that leg, Miss Farnell! *Move* it, and keep that circulation going. Most important that you keep it moving. Got to clear that clot, you know!'

'I would like to clear *her* clot,' Anna said to Dominic, 'by doing a double *grand jeté* upon her thick skull!'

'Anna, have a heart. The girl's only doing her job.'

Anna kept attending because she had no real choice; James insisted upon it.

'I've been exercising both my legs since I was six years old!' she protested. 'The woman is so ridiculously enthusiastic she's unreal.'

James laughed. 'I'm afraid it tends to run in the trade. But do keep it up; she knows her stuff. I want this thing cleared up without resorting to surgery, and so do you.'

That was unanswerable, so Anna went faithfully; she submitted to Roberta's ham-fisted attempts at encouragement with good grace, and grimaced inwardly, and got on with it.

She didn't like it. No one had said she had to like it. On the mornings she was due at hospital Anna dawdled; if Jason had been alive to see he would have called it her 'reluctant' look; he would have laughed at her, with her.

Jason was dead. That was final; every time it crossed her mind it left a bleak, grey trace of heartache.

Anna seldom read a newspaper, and she wasn't really reading her father's, that morning. She would have learned sooner or later of the news contained in the item which caught her eye, no doubt; seeing it that morning, unprepared for it, gave her a shock.

She found it in the gossip column for which the paper was famous and which was largely credited for its huge circulation.

The article was crisply written, slightly sarcastic in the style of the transatlantic journalist who had written it.

Steven Harwood, Nabob of the Royal Ballet, has recently shown himself the possessor of an unexpectedly soft heart.

Failing the services of dancer Dominic Lautrec—on leave of absence due to what Harwood chooses to describe as illness in Mr Lautrec's family, but more probably due to the illness of Mr Lautrec's live-in lover and partner, ailing dancer Anna Farnell—Harwood has cast Claude Antonini in the fattest role in his Christmas production of Tearoses, *vaunted as the important new work of Ms June Bellini, borrowed from New York especially for the season.*

One hopes Mr Antonini equal to the part. One hopes for Mr Lautrec's return to his Company with all possible speed.

That was all. The column continued with notes about other famous people; the readership was wide, and there were lots of strings to the journalist's bow.

It was enough.

Dominic was eating toast, unconcerned, relaxed, planning strategies to hustle Anna out of her dressing gown and into her clothes, if she didn't make a move very soon. She looked up and watched him for a moment, loving him for the way a shaft of morning sunlight caught his dark, shining hair, for what he had tried to do for her, simply for the way he ate toast.

'You didn't tell me about *Tearoses*, Dominic. You said the Christmas season was to be *Nutcracker*, run-of-the-mill stuff.'

'Well, I—'

'You didn't tell me because you knew I'd insist you go back to London for it.'

'Anna, we've been through all this. There will be other *Tearoses*, other seasons.'

Other ballets, other opportunities Dominic would opt out of. Because of her. Other white lies, hesitations when she pleaded with him to go, to fly in spite of her . . . because of her.

He was ambitious, or at least he had been; ambition was a vital part of the equipment of star quality.

He might grow tired of her, tired of walking slowly to keep pace with her when all the people he worked with were vitally healthy, whole, bursting with energy and enthusiasm and joy in the common goal of dancing.

But it was worse than that. Oh, she knew she could keep him by her side all her life long, faithful, devoted, loving . . . and by doing that she would be responsible for cramping a great talent.

'You've turned your back on your career. You can't do that. Not even for one season.'

'Anna, for God's sake, we've been over all this before! I love you, and that's more important to me than a chance to perform the bloody starring part in *Tearoses* or any other damned ballet!'

She very nearly laughed. It was the way he said 'bloody' with his slight French inflection. It came out as 'bluuudy'. She didn't laugh.

She wanted him, wanted to be with him no matter whatever in the world might happen, for always. But if she indulged herself, permitted him to go on always thinking of her, loving her, it would be the most selfish thing she had ever done. She couldn't bear it.

It had niggled at her from somewhere in her innermost depths, bothered her through all the weeks she suspected, then knew as a certainty, that she couldn't go back to the Company with him as his partner.

'I want you to go back to London, Dominic.'

'I will darling. After Christmas—'

'No. "After Christmas" was a pipe dream, a little fiction we made up to fool ourselves. Before we . . . knew. There—is—no—after—Christmas for us, Dominic. You must go now. I want you to go now.'

He stared at her aghast, holding her eyes with his; she thought she might faint, or scream, or simply go into his arms and sob until her heart broke in half. Instead she took a breath and steadied her voice, and tried as she'd never tried in her life before to make her words convincing. 'I want you to send my things to me from the flat. Send them, please, don't bring them. I want you to clear out and stay out, do you understand?'

'No. I don't.'

'Well, you must try. I know your sense of duty has kept you here, and—'

'What!'

Anna lifted a hand to her eyes as though to shield them from a sight too painful to watch.

Dominic's knuckles were white on the edge of the table. He pushed himself to his feet and went to her side; he tried to take her into his arms.

She wrenched away, gritting her teeth against the desire to turn to him, bury her face in him, to claim him and keep him by her side for all the rest of their lives.

She longed to go back, back to the days when they were truly together, when they had . . . dazzled the world . . . together.

She longed to hold him, totally exhausted but far too excited to think about sleeping, while they read the reviews of their latest performance in the early papers.

She longed to be with him at those awful parties after the premières, to see the lifted eyebrow that meant they might slip out unnoticed for food, and then a long walk, and then a deep, dreamless sleep after making love. And to awaken knowing that he was there beside her, and that the next day would hold the same promises for them—the excitement, the performances, the exhaustion, the private world of just the two of them, the joy of it.

Dancing, dancing, and living together; laughing, loving, working together. That had been their life, and it was gone.

Anna remembered the first time he had asked her to go out with him in Paris . . . the dinner beneath the chandeliers that swung from trees . . . the laughter of that first summer, and the night he had kissed her for the first time. They had been as one, two people living a magical mirror of the roles they danced. That was gone now, all gone.

'Don't you love me, Anna?' Dominic whispered, anguished.

She opened her mouth, but the sound she made was the whimper of a hurt, frightened child.

He tried again to take her into his arms; again she wrenched away, determined to control herself, determined to find the words which would send him away from her. Back to where he belonged.

'I . . . I don't love you as I did,' she said.

'I don't believe you.'

She closed her eyes. 'It's true.'

The coffee and the toast were cold, the sun gone in behind a sudden cloud. Anna rose, and tightened the sash of her dressing gown around her waist. The restless gesture would protect her, keep her from reaching out to him.

'Anna . . .?'

She shook her head quickly. 'You have to believe me, Dominic. I want you to go. Now, today.' Her voice was flat, dead; his eyes were unreadable, and he stood very still.

'Anna, we must talk about this.'

'There's nothing—'

'Anna, Anna, we have so much, so very much. Don't throw it away, Anna. Please don't throw it away.'

He walked to her and she went into his arms. It was so good, so easy; she could stay there always, the rest of their lives.

He kissed the top of her head, and stroked her hair. She ached for him, wanted him as she had never done before. She had taken the love for granted, never dreaming it would come to anything so painful.

At last and with great effort she disentangled herself from his embrace and stood back, steeled herself to look into his eyes. It was for the best. To send him away. For his good, for the good of his career.

'Dominic, what—what we had together is . . . gone. There isn't enough left to—to make it work.'

She couldn't dance, couldn't dance. Dominic could, and he must. Without her. Without a millstone. Free. Free.

'No! Anna—'

'Yes, Dominic. When I come back from hospital today, I want you to have gone. Back to London. Back to the Company.'

'Why, Anna? Just tell me why?'

She clenched her fists at her sides, fighting against the desire to go into his arms again. 'I told you,' she said woodenly. 'I don't love you . . . as I did.'

'You really *mean* that?'

She nodded, unable to speak, unable to trust her voice to say the carefully-rehearsed lies yet again.

Pain and shock mixed with disbelief in his dark eyes; his shoulders slumped, his arms hung at his sides.

Anna turned away from him and left the room. She was trying not to run, and she was shaking, all the forces of her heart, her soul, at war with what she was doing to him, to both of them. What she felt she had to do.

She reached the stairs before the first sob tore from her throat. She stumbled and grabbed the banister to steady herself, to make herself put one foot in front of the other up the stairs to her room.

Somehow she managed to dress herself in brown slacks and an old green jumper, loafers; somehow she managed to go back down the stairs and out of the house. Mercifully, Dominic didn't follow her, nor did he attempt to speak to her again.

Anna took a bus to hospital, endured the pathologists and Roberta; when that was finished, she spun out more time sitting with cooling tea and cigarettes in a café. When she went home again, Dominic was gone.

He left no note, but in her vase there was a fresh, fragrant, long-stemmed rose, red as blood. She picked up the vase and held it to her rapidly-beating heart so tightly that the delicate crystal splintered in her hands.

She wept then, with the pain in her cut hands and with the pain which seemed to spread in an ugly, hopeless spiral from the depths of her very being. Then she threw herself onto her bed, still vaguely scented with Dominic's cologne, and sobbed as if she would never stop.

CHAPTER FOURTEEN

Steven Harwood wrote a beautiful note in reply to Anna's resignation. Even the paper he used was in impeccably good taste; it was heavy, folded once, with a simple line drawing on the front.

He offered her his best wishes and any practical help he could provide, whenever she might come to him. He did not refer to her brutally abrupt estrangement from Dominic Lautrec. If he knew about it (and Mikhail Niroff almost certainly had seen to it that they all did) he made no reference to it even indirectly. That would have been rude, prying, as unlike Steven as it was possible to be.

By the end of November the blood clot in Anna's vein dispersed spontaneously; though her leg was still weak, most of the residual swelling had gone, and she was less often troubled by pain.

'You're nearly good as new,' James said.

'Nearly. I still can't dance.'

'But you had other plans, Anna. Plans to take a studio in London and teach, and—'

'Those weren't really plans. They were daydreams: pleasant, meaningless.'

'They sounded fairly solid at the time. Anna, why did you send Dominic away like that?'

'I've already told you.'

'Not really.'

Anna's voice was toneless as she answered, as if her speech had been learned off by heart and rehearsed to herself in the mirror many, many times.

'He turned down the leading male role in an important new ballet just so he could be with me at Christmas. He couldn't go on doing things like that, not without wrecking a great career. I sent him away. It wouldn't have worked out.'

'You sound like a tape recorder, Anna.'

'Well?'

'You didn't give it a chance. And you're unhappy without him, I can see that.'

'So what? Who isn't unhappy, most of the time?'

James looked at her. Anna was listless, losing weight.

Once she had been so fully occupied with class, rehearsals, performing, that she could think of a million things she wanted to do if she had only had the time. Now time had been thrust upon her, and she had no idea what to do with it, to occupy a spirit too low to care.

James saw all that very clearly, yet there seemed little he could do about it.

'Shall I buy you a coffee before you go home? Or better still, what would you say to lunch?'

'You're trying to cheer me up.' Her voice was toneless.

'Guilty, but it's worth a try. I'll make it even more tempting. We'll give Ye Olde Copper Kettle a miss and drive out along the river road to that snazzy-looking wine bar they've put into the old bakehouse at Radleigh Cross. I haven't been there yet.'

Anna had, with Dominic.

The disused Victorian bakehouse was at the end of a row of shops along the main street of what had once been a small but thriving village; in recent years its population had dwindled steadily, and many of its buildings had fallen into nearly total dereliction. Its cottages were old, of stone and daub or brick. Most of them had been allowed to sink into sad, abandoned disrepair.

Radleigh Cross was saved, miraculously, almost overnight. When the new town of Elmwood Centre was built, the little village was gradually peopled by the young, trendy, affluent executives of new town industry who wouldn't dream of housing their families on one of the new estates.

They wanted cottages, albeit with modernized kitchens and central heating, but cottages just the same, the older the better; they wanted to resurrect the village school, and to give their children idyllic Kate Greenaway childhoods in the fresh country air.

Within a year of the construction of most of Elmwood Centre, all the remotely habitable buildings in Radleigh Cross had been bought up at give-away prices and lovingly restored; one or two of the oldest buildings had even been placed under the protection of preservation orders.

The village bustled, prospered and throbbed with an energy it had never before known in all its long, sleepy life. There was a health food shop in what had once been the fishmonger's, a craft and antique arcade along the old stone-paved street that led down to the river.

There was also a branch bank, an ordinary grocery shop, a launderette, a petrol station, and a newsagent's, but most of the serious shopping was done elsewhere by the new villagers, in Pendleton or further afield in one of the massive supermarkets in Elmwood Centre's shopping district.

Radleigh Cross was intended as a showcase of updated country life, and soon its gentrification was complete.

The new owners of the bakehouse had done an impressive job on their Victorian building, restoring it carefully so that its original function was clear, incorporated into the new decor: the massive brick ovens which lined two of its walls were left intact, as were the smoke-stained beams in its low ceilings. The tables and chairs were in harmony with the building too, bare and plain and wooden, oases of privacy beneath clever lighting.

It was popular from the day it opened, crowded every lunchtime and then again in the evening by people who had enough money and sufficient experience to be bored by pub grub, or the bland and stodgy offerings of fish and chips and Anglicized Chinese take-away.

Dominic had taken Anna there many times, marvelling at the wine list and the quality of the food.

'Why do you find it so special?' she had teased. 'It's only a wine bar, after all.'

'Oh well yes, of course it is. But to think of finding pickled mushrooms and respectable quiche in the middle of Buckinghamshire!'

Dominic loved the village too. Sometimes they had spent a Saturday afternoon just strolling around it. Once they stopped to peer into the window of a shop so small they nearly passed it; Dominic spotted a doll there, the kind with a china head and a painted face and garish, billowing green satin skirts. He insisted upon buying it for Anna. She still had it in her room, carefully hidden in a drawer.

She nearly declined James' invitation, but changed her mind.

It would be painful to be in Radleigh Cross, painful to sit in the wine bar remembering Dominic's face, his delighted laughter, his hand reaching across the table for hers. But she knew she couldn't go on trying to avoid all the places which would remind her of him.

There were too many of them.

Helen didn't know what to say to Anna, or even if she should try to say anything at all. She was still wrestling with her own raw grief for her son, and the fact that Christmas was nearly upon them made it all seem very much worse.

The carollers were out some nights, singing the familiar songs. The most festive of them pulled at the heartstrings, but the joyfully sentimental carols were enough to send Helen dashing to her bedroom before Martin or Anna could catch up with her, sobbing as if her heart were a bit of shattered glass that could never be mended.

The shops were full of it too, full of the magazine annuals and the chocolate bars in net Christmas stockings which had been Jason's stubborn attachments to an outgrown childhood, gifts he requested shamelessly, year after year.

There were the coloured lights along the High Street which he loved so much, and the corny, glitter-sprinkled Christmas cards he invariably sent to all his friends.

It was everywhere, all around her; Helen could barely manage to make her way around the Co-op to do her daily shopping without her chin quivering at the sight of the satsumas and walnuts and crackers on the shelves, the relentless, tinny sound of canned Christmas music that followed her up and down the aisles until at last she could pay at the till and bolt for home.

Helen was worried about Anna. She knew that Martin must be worried too. She and Martin had a close marriage, a strong one, but they had never been the kind of people to talk much together, or to try to analyze the events of life.

They loved one another, they loved their children when they came. They had always expressed the love more in little, daily ways than in words. But the weight of this tragedy was too heavy for that; somehow Helen felt that by putting it into words she might be able to reduce it, force it to a manageable size. She would have to try.

Finally one night in bed she turned to Martin.

'What . . . can we do about Anna, love?'

He sat up in bed and switched on his table lamp, and reached over to take her into his arms. He hadn't been asleep. He had been lying there beside his wife, wondering how to shape the words to ask her the same thing.

'I don't think I know what we can do. I still don't understand why she sent Dominic away, for a start. I even tried asking her about it outright, but that was no bloody good. She doesn't say much, does she?'

'No . . . no, she doesn't. He rang again today, did I tell you?'

Dominic rang every day without fail, and had done so since the day he left Pendleton. Anna couldn't bear to speak to him; she knew that if she heard his voice she would weaken and plead with him to come back to her. He would come, she knew that, on the first possible train. And then they would be back where they were before the inexpressibly painful day she had sent him away. She refused to speak to him.

And he wrote to her. So many letters.

The first letter he sent jolted Anna badly, as she recognized his handwriting on the envelope. The return address in the corner was the London flat where they'd shared so much happiness.

Anna took the letter and ran to her room, the room which had been theirs. She sat down on their bed, and ran the flat of one hand longingly over the neat script in which Dominic had written her name.

She sat for an hour holding it crushed against her breast, not able to bring herself to open it. At last, cramped and stiff, she rose. She buried the letter beneath some photographs in her bureau drawer.

All that day the letter nagged at her, pulled at her like a magnet; it would say 'I love you', she knew that. Dominic would be telling her that they belonged together no matter what.

Oh, God help her, what could she say to that? She had to try to be strong, but she felt no strength; she felt only the gnawing, miserable certainty that life without him was a colourless string of empty days, emptier nights.

Sometimes she awoke in the night, stifling her gulping sobs with a fist for fear her parents would hear her; she would have been dreaming of Dominic, the dream a clear and simple scene from out of their past: running through the Paris streets together, or eating lunch, laughing, happy. Most often she dreamed of being in his arms, dancing or just . . . being in his arms.

She would have given anything to go back, back to the blissful serenity of loving him and being loved; she would have given anything, but she knew she had to be strong for him, for the sake of his career.

When Dominic's second letter came, Anna got out the first. With an unsteady hand she crossed out her address and returned them both, unopened. He continued to write to her; she continued to return the letters.

The flowers were worse, living reminders of Dominic's love.

The single rose he had left her on the day she sent him away had torn her apart; he had always given her roses. He sent a dozen, a few days after she had returned his first two letters. They were perfect; their fragrance evocative of so much they had shared. Holding them was almost . . . almost like holding Dominic to her heart.

Anna buried her face deeply in their perfume, and when she looked up there were teardrops on the delicate petals.

She had to thank him for the flowers, thank him in such a way that she would convince him once and for always that she couldn't run to him, cling to him, hold him back.

She had to try to put a full stop to their love, because . . . because . . .

Holding her pen, trying to shape the words on paper, Anna felt she couldn't go on. She ran a trembling hand through her hair and gazed through her window at the barren trees, trying hard to remember why it was so important to end the love which meant the world to her, which was her life.

She bit her lip and stared down at what she had written. It was a lie, all of it, a stiff and formal little death knell to all their hopes and plans. It was a necessary lie, stiff and formal and distant.

'Dear Dominic,
Thank you for the flowers.'

Oh but please, if you love me, for God's sake don't send me flowers. Oh Dominic, Dominic, it hurts too much . . .

'. . . it is for the best that we parted. I am feeling stronger now, and hope to make a new life here. I wish you all the very best in the world.'

All the very best, my love, singing in the misty rain of a Paris dawn, or in the London flat, going out with your anorak over your pyjama tops to buy fresh croissants and the early papers, or shouting 'I'm starving' after a performance. I won't be there with you, and there will be an empty place in my heart as long as I live, but . . . I wish you . . . all the very best. I love you so.

She sealed the note and went out to post it, and everything she didn't say was engraved on her heart.

Later Anna arranged the roses in Helen's best vase, and placed them on the bureau in her parents' bedroom. Helen said 'Thank you, dear,' as though to encourage Anna to share the anguish that burned in her eyes.

Anna said nothing; she merely smiled, and shook her head. After that, whenever the flowers came for Anna, she handed them to her mother without a word.

Steven Harwood sighed, and looked across at Dominic.

'I accepted Anna's resignation.' He spread his hands helplessly. 'I had no choice.'

Dominic ran a hand over his face, across his eyes as though to clear them. 'So did I, I suppose. I didn't have a choice either.'

The older man coughed behind his hand, nervous, embarrassed. He had heard something of it, from Niroff, though Steven disliked gossip intensely and was loath to pay attention to it; gossip could create havoc in a dancing company.

'Is there anything I can do?' Steven's voice was quiet, serious. He was painfully torn between his personal feelings for these two magical children, Anna and Dominic, and his real worries over what the cruel loss of the partnership might mean to the Company. He couldn't afford to lose both of them.

'No, Steven,' Dominic said. 'There's nothing anyone can do. I can go on working, though. Don't worry on that score. It's all that's left.'

'I'm . . . sorry.'

'Thank you, Steven.' Dominic lit a cigarette and drew deeply on it, his slender fingers fanning his mouth, his eyes sombre. 'I love her so very much . . . you know?'

'I think I do, Dominic. I'm sorry,' he said again.

'Did she speak to him, Helen?'

Helen shook her head, and brushed angrily at her eyes. 'I suppose she thinks she's done the right and proper thing, sending him back to his work. But they'd made so many plans. You remember, he'd even got her convinced she could teach in London, and that they could carry on as they were.'

'What happened to all that?' Martin asked.

'Dominic told me that he'd been . . . evasive with her, about the Company's programme for the Christmas season. When she found out he'd turned down a big part in it she was angry with him, said he was telling lies, and told him to go back and do it . . . without her.'

'She still cares for him, though.'

'Oh, of course she does! People don't switch their feelings off and on like electric lights. You know that.'

'Well, perhaps in time—'

'No, Martin, I don't think so. She seems as if she's . . . sinking, day to day. She feels as badly as we do over Jason, only—worse. I think she feels guilty because he died.'

They all did. That feeling stirred and floated periodically into every one of their hearts, beside or beneath the grief, a part of it. Of everyone involved, however, James's perception of his guilt was clearest, easiest to deal with because at least he was aware of it.

He delved into Jason's medical records and studied them for hours, patiently piecing together the string of events which had apparently led to the boy's illness, and then to his death.

At the bottom of it all, or so it seemed, were the steroids and penicillamine prescribed in combination to ease his arthritic condition. The treatment might have triggered the anaemia though studying further even that wasn't establishable beyond the shadow of a doubt.

Tears

Aplastic anaemia could occur spontaneously; it might have done so in Jason. No one could ever be absolutely sure, not even the pathologists.

His death from the disease was no one's fault; Chandler's management of the team of consultants and nurses involved had been meticulously careful. The graft-versus-host complication which had been the direct cause of death was not always possible to prevent, unless the marrow donor was the recipient's identical twin. And once the donor's graft began to fight the patient it was hellishly difficult to treat. Chandler had done his very best; they all had.

Anna's thrombosis had been no one's fault either. It happened sometimes after surgery; unfortunately it had happened to Anna Farnell.

That left James very firmly at square one, with everybody off the hook and nobody to blame. It would have been easier all round if there had been; then at least they could point to the culprit and direct the corrosive guilt away from their own hearts.

James dealt with his own irrational guilt methodically and scientifically, as a doctor was trained to do. Having dealt with it, he was free to assume the task of helping the Farnells, as their doctor and their friend.

Martin and Helen went together to the surgery.

'We don't like talking about this behind Anna's back,' Martin said. 'But neither of us knows what to do, or how to cope. She's unhappy, James, muddled up in her feelings.'

'She won't talk about it much though, will she?'

Helen shook her head, twisting her handkerchief in her hands. 'I keep thinking it's my fault, really. I've been so miserable—and Christmas makes it almost . . . unbearable. I keep thinking that once we get through

Christmas, things will take a turn for the better.'

'It isn't your fault, Helen. Nor Martin's, nor anyone's. I've gone over every jot on Jason's records, and I'm convinced that when it comes right down to cases, there simply isn't anyone to blame for what happened. As for Anna, I've been puzzled myself about how to help her over the worst of it. She feels responsible, I'm certain. A part of her blames herself because she couldn't save Jason's life, and that doesn't help. On top of all that, there's her deep frustration at not being able to dance. Has she said anything recently about teaching?'

'No,' Helen said. 'I tried asking her about that, but she made it clear she didn't want to discuss it. And she won't talk about Dominic. She refuses to speak to him on the telephone, or even to read his letters. I feel so . . . helpless. It isn't that she's thoughtless or anything like that. Now she's getting well, she's doing everything she can to help me. She even goes out shopping for me, so I won't have to . . . see the tinsel in the shops . . .'

'I tried to get her to open up,' Martin said. 'It wasn't any use. She's mindful of my feelings too, about the way I feel over losing Jason. But it's as though she's decided she can't have any feelings of her own.'

James answered with more cheer than he felt. 'We'll just have to jostle her out of it, then, won't we?'

It was going to take time. Time and tact and skill—and a little bit of luck.

James thought about Christmas.

The season had sad associations for him too. He had loved, had made a family, had gamely praised his young wife's first ham-fisted attempt at mince pies.

He knew all too well what agony it was going to be for the Farnells this year, and he thought about it very carefully. They had relatives they could go to; he knew that. But the Farnells' relatives had families of their own, still intact; any of them would have welcomed Martin and Helen and Anna warmly, and would have done their best to include them in the feast.

That was the trouble: there would be feasts anywhere they went, anticipated and lovingly-planned for months. And even if they joined a household in which the children had grown up and moved away, there would be grandchildren, their eyes aglow with the wonder of it all.

At best the Farnells would be fussed over, worried over until they wished they hadn't come; at worst the unbridled joy of laughing children would remind them of what they had lost.

'I'm not much cop as a cook, Helen,' James said, 'but I'm more than willing to have a bash. Why don't you lot come to me for Christmas this year?'

'Oh James no, it's far too much—'

'Nonsense. Do me good to play host for a change.'

He wanted the three of them out of their own house, on Christmas Day and Boxing Day as well; the ghost of Christmas Past clanked so loudly in a house of sorrow. James planned the two days of intensive seasonal festivity with careful restraint.

They exchanged small gifts late on Christmas morning: not to do that much would merely have underlined their loss.

They formed a chain of hands around James's table when they sat down to the roast beef he'd prepared, surprisingly well, for a man who said he couldn't cook. Martin offered a short grace and mentioned Jason, and it seemed to all of them more of a comfort than if he had not.

On Boxing Day James proposed a long drive and a ramble through a railway museum he himself wanted to visit. He'd feared it might be boring for the others, but it wasn't. Afterwards they stopped at a nearby pub for lunch.

That—apart from two visits to mutual friends when they returned to Pendleton—was Christmas safely dealt with.

Or almost. Dominic sent an extravagant spray of roses to Anna on Christmas Eve. There was a note attached to it; her hands trembled as she opened it. 'I love you.'

He sent a poinsettia to Helen and Martin.

Anna's painfully mending heart broke afresh.

The previous Christmas she and Dominic had been together, in London. They had been frantically busy, dancing the traditional *Nutcracker* to enraptured audiences, right up to the matinée on Christmas Eve. Even so, Dominic had found the time to surprise her with a small tree for the flat, which they decorated with hastily-purchased ornaments.

At the last minute he had bundled her off with him to Pendleton.

'We must offer your family the greetings of the season,' he said, 'and present Jason with his special gift.'

'Oh, of course!' she had answered, her eyes sparkling. 'He wouldn't be able to live without it.'

It was a tee-shirt luridly stencilled with glittering Batman and Robin figures, totally inappropriate for any occasion except perhaps a fun-fair. Jason had loved it.

There had been French *bonbons* for Helen from Dominic's mother, for Martin hand-rolled cigars.

Anna had given Dominic a pair of cufflinks in white gold, and she had gasped when she opened his gift to her: it was a ring, a delicate filigree of silver strands capturing a small, exquisite amethyst. She had blushed as he fitted it onto her ring finger, looking up at him through the fringes of her lashes.

'Is it meant—?'

Tears

'To be an engagement ring? If you want it to be, *chérie*.' He had tilted her chin in his hand and kissed her. 'Though I had planned your engagement ring to be a diamond *this* big.' He made an extravagant gesture with both hands.

She laughed at him and shook her head, and for all that day and the days that followed she wore the ring everywhere, refusing to part with it.

After the turkey of Christmas afternoon it snowed; Anna and Dominic trooped out together to pelt one another with sparse snowballs, laughing until they cried, their gloves and coats and shoes completely soaked.

After Boxing Day Anna and Dominic had returned to London, to work, to dance.

And on New Year's Eve they had stayed at home, sharing a bottle of champagne to toast their glittering future, admiring their little tree, wrapped in the exhilaration, the exhaustion that always came after work, loving every minute of it, loving one another.

And now Anna's world was flat, grey, and all the carefree happiness was gone. Forever.

For once, Anna couldn't bear to give Dominic's flowers to her mother. She took them to her own room, put them carefully into a vase, and placed it on top of her bureau. Then she set aside just one exquisite bud while she opened the top drawer of her bureau. She found the small velvet box with its silver filigree ring inside.

She took out the ring with tender care. She slipped in onto her finger and kissed it and thought of Dominic laughing, loving her.

She picked up the rosebud and slipped it gently beneath her pillow, to dream on.

There was no future for them now, Anna knew that. But it was Christmas, and she could dream.

She wore the ring to bed; she kept the rosebud beneath her pillow. A few days later it was withered and flat. She couldn't bear to throw it away. She pressed it carefully between the pages of a book of sonnets.

> 'A heart once broken is a heart no more,
> And is excused from all a heart must be...'

Anna wept.

CHAPTER FIFTEEN

'You're fit! Perfect blood counts at last.'

'Fit for what?'

'Oh dear, here we have a case of the wobbly doldrums. If you were ten years younger I could treat that with sugar pills. Remember those?'

Anna smiled in spite of her detemination not to allow James to humour her.

'Like Roberta. Any minute now you'll go off into orbit like Mary Poppins, whistling a happy tune.'

But she did remember sugar pills. Dr Rogerson had given them to every child he treated, blithely unconcerned—or perhaps not quite modern enough to know—about the dental outrage which would eventually banish them from every surgery, even those of simple country doctors.

'Now, what are you going to do with the rest of your life?'

She shrugged.

'Seriously, I mean it. Nobody can mope forever, Anna. There's no reason on earth why you shouldn't be up and doing.'

'James . . . I would stop—moping, if only I could. I can't seem to manage it.'

A month had passed since Christmas.

Dun, rainy January had brought nothing with it save the Tuesday post, regular as clock-work, in which Anna received her sickness benefit.

That, and flowers from Dominic. Roses.

It had got to the point where Anna clenched her teeth every time the doorbell rang and avoided answering it whenever she could.

The bittersweet pain of receiving Dominic's flowers had become worse for her over the months instead of easing. Anna could picture him in the tiny florist's shop in Covent Garden, choosing them with deliberate care to make sure they were perfect; delicate messengers of his love.

Sometimes Anna held conversations with him in her head, pleading with him to stop sending them, pleading with him to understand that now she couldn't dance beside him she no longer had a place in his life—that they couldn't ever again be together, that she would only hold him back.

But when the flowers came less often, when Dominic rang less often, when his letters all but stopped, the pain was worse.

Alone at night in her room, Anna sometimes felt she would go out of her mind with the anguish of it; she sat for hours on her bed, rocking herself, staring into space, trying to understand why she had been singled out for the crushing blow of losing everything which once had been her life.

She read in a trade journal that Dominic had been invited to dance in Milan in the spring, that the Christmas season in London he had joined at the eleventh hour was astonishingly successful for him and everyone else involved in it.

She supposed she should be proud that she had sacrificed—well, what? Only her own selfish desire to cling to him, to drain him until there was nothing left.

At night in her room, when no one could see her, surrounded by mementoes—the chain he had given her for her twenty-second birthday, her filigree ring, her pressed flowers—Anna felt abandoned, numb. She wanted him. She yearned for him with such an intensity that it was all she could do not to pick up the telephone and tell him so.

Anna cashed her sickness benefit each week at the post office and banked it around the corner. It wasn't much, but she didn't need much.

Her parents wouldn't hear of taking a share of her money.

'The mortgage was paid off last year, love,' her father mumbled, embarrassed when she tried to insist. 'And goodness knows you've not been eating much. You save that money for the studio you'll need, and for the equipment you'll be wanting when you set up teaching, or . . . whatever you decide to do. If you've not got enough near the time, we'll help all we can.'

Anna knew she ought to do something; she could see the worry in her parents' eyes, sense the whispered conferences with James. She felt she was letting them all down, giving in to self-pity and wasting what she might easily salvage from the years of work and study. But still, she couldn't force herself to act.

Her days were spent in a curious, empty echo of the days of her childhood, before she had gone away to study ballet. She didn't go to school, but in almost every other way it was the same. Perhaps more like an endless string of the Saturdays she spent at home when she was young.

She got up in the morning, dressed, ate breakfast, helped Helen with the laundry and the housework; then, usually together now, they'd go along to the shops.

Helen would stand dithering, slightly perplexed, just as Anna could remember her all those years ago:

'Shall we have ham and salad, dear, or perhaps a nice bit of steak?'

Anna's world had shrunk to a few homely, remembered routines, narrowed until some days it seemed that she *was* ten again. Or rather six or seven before Jason had been born.

The friends of her own age she might have made in Pendleton had grown up without her, gone to local schools, left the town or married people she didn't know; Anna had spent her entire adolescence comparing notes on stance and deportment and the correct angle of a pointed foot with girls and boys in London.

Occasionally she turned to James Harrington for comfort. He understood something of what had happened to her life, and he was prepared to help her to pick up the pieces now that nothing much was left of it.

'Just think about teaching, Anna, that's all I ask. You might find it quite a challenge, and you'd have no trouble finding pupils.'

'I can't go back to London. I can't. Dom— There are too many memories there, too many reminders.'

'All right then, why not teach right here?'

'Here? In Pendleton?'

He laughed. 'I know it's a bit provincial, but I'll bet they'd be queueing up before the ink was dry on your advert., just waiting to get a chance to strut in front of a real professional.'

'You really think so?'

'Didn't you take ballet lessons here yourself, before you went to White Lodge?' He had her interest now, he could feel it. He pressed on. 'They don't all have to have world-beating talent, you know. A bit of ballet training never hurt any child. Good for the posture.'

And so, at last, Anna began to think about it. It was true Helen had enrolled her for lessons with a local dancing teacher long before there had been any thought of auditioning for a serious stage boarding-school.

She could still remember the thrill of pride she felt in her first headband and real ballet slippers, the carefully pressed practice tunic; the excitement when recital evening came at last and Anna danced her first solo performance, carefully coached by Mrs Griggs.

Mrs Griggs was an old woman then; she had died shortly after her retirement. It was one of Anna's deep regrets that her teacher had never seen her dancing on the London stage. She would have burst with the joy of it.

Mrs Griggs herself had never performed. But she was an accredited ballet teacher, and she knew her job. Her eyes had shone with delight the day she had sent for Anna's parents to tell them with an unsuppressed trill of absolute assurance that their daughter should go further with her dancing than she could ever take her.

'You'd find premises easily enough, Anna,' James was saying. 'Here in town, why not? Pendleton's on all the bus routes from Elmwood Centre, so you'd attract custom from the whole shooting match.'

'But I'm not qualified . . . to teach.'

James was on the Farnells' doorstep the following morning, holding several authoritative-looking books on classical ballet. Helen knew something was going on; she made her excuses and disappeared up the stairs to leave the two of them to talk.

'It says here,' James said, spreading out the books on the kitchen table, 'and here—*and* here, that the qualifications required to teach classical ballet can be acquired from a teachers' training course, *or* from professional experience. You've got that, Anna.'

She looked up into his eager face and smiled. He must be well over thirty. But he was trying so hard to help her, and in his enthusiasm he looked so much like a raw-boned, overgrown schoolboy she wanted to hug him.

He had done so much for her, for all of them, suffering with them through their tragedy; he'd tried to give them a nearly painless Christmas, he'd listened to her for hours, he'd been there, always, when they needed him.

Anna knew by then about James's own personal tragedy, the wife and baby who'd died. He'd suffered too, but he'd overcome it; he'd decided to go on living. So would she. Or try to.

'All right, James, you win. I'll read the books, and I'll think about it really seriously.' She grinned. 'I'll even give you a cup of coffee.'

CHAPTER SIXTEEN

Dominic sat tailor-fashion on the floor of the Crush Bar upstairs at Covent Garden, sharing a take-away fried chicken dinner with Claude Antonini between a frantic rehearsal and an evening performance.

'Thirty-seven secret herbs and spices, bah!'

'It's food,' Claude said.

'I suppose so. God knows we need something to keep ourselves going in this non-stop carnival. Christ, when are we going to get decent rehearsal space? In Paris—'

'Oh, come off it, Dominic. Stop bitching and eat your chicken. Here, have a beer.'

Dominic was working hard, working well, dancing all the plum roles and collecting lots of glory, making a reputation with something approaching the speed of light. He was going to make it, really make it big; he deserved to, and Claude wished him well.

But ever since he'd come back to London at Christmas he'd been driving himself as though demons were after him. Claude had known him long enough to try to get him to cool it every so often.

Sure it was hectic, having to rehearse in the theatre bar because they were so cramped back-stage, and sure the meals were snatched at the busiest times, but so what? They were dancers; no one had ever promised them a cushy number.

Claude was getting a big boost out of Dominic's chain of successes. He knew that, and he was grateful for it. He wasn't in the same class as a dancer, and he knew that too. But he was working on it, and when Dominic was invited away from the Company, Claude and a few of the other male principals would have a chance at the plum roles.

All that was fine. The only thing that really niggled Claude was Nicole Girard. She was Dominic's London partner now, more often than not, ever since Anna had got sick. Nicole wasn't in the same class as Anna, not yet, but she seemed to be working night and day, and she was getting better all the time.

There had been a brief period when Claude thought he might be getting somewhere with Nicole, but when Dominic came back from wherever it was he'd been holding Anna's hand, Dominic had taken over—plum roles, Nicole's undivided attention and all.

'What do you hear from Anna?'

'Not a goddamned thing. She doesn't want to know me now. She can't dance, and therefore she feels the noble, the correct course of action is to spit me out like the pip of a grape. *Voilà!* No dancing, no Lautrec!'

'Nicole seems pretty keen.'

Dominic shrugged indifferently. 'She works hard, she's getting more polished, more controlled.'

'And—personally?'

Claude was probing, feeling his way in an effort to find out how far Nicole had replaced Anna Farnell.

Dominic looked at him thoughtfully. 'You're interested in Nicole, right?'

Claude concentrated on the debris of the take-away meal, gathering crumpled paper and beer cans into the cardboard carton.

'Well?'

Claude didn't look up.

'Come on, man, it's written all over you.'

'Yeah, okay. So?'

'I advise you to forget it. Concentrate on your elevation. Keep thinking about that motionless stance when you've completed a lift. That will get you further—'

'Balls, mate! What do you think I am, some kind of bleeding nancy-boy? There's a life to be lived off-stage too, you know.'

Dominic sighed and shook his head. 'Look, Claude, I promise you I have no more romantic interest in Nicole than I have in the usherettes who count tickets at the door. I'm . . . okay, I'm bitter.'

'She fancies you,' Claude said.

'I doubt it. Nicole fancies her chances of making her name as a ballerina. That's the sum total of her interest in me, I'm sure.'

Claude wasn't.

He had taken her out a few times while Dominic was away, had nearly but not quite worn down her flirtatious resistance to going back to his flat afterwards, to bed. At the last minute she always turned him down, but still it looked as though with time—

Now, when she looked in Claude's direction there wasn't so much as a hint of promise in her eyes.

The critics were increasingly charmed with her. They even soft-pedalled their comparisons of her work with that of the vanished, lamented Anna Farnell. They approved of Nicole's Giselle, tolerated her Aurora, and were openly admiring of the stunning technique she sometimes managed to achieve in the newer, modern works—works like *Tearoses*, at Christmas. That had earned her a cautious rave or two.

Dominic knew she would improve; he would help her all he could. But she would never be another Anna Farnell. He could feel a lack of fluidity when he partnered her, a want of what for lack of a better word Dominic thought of as 'soul'.

But she was working hard on everything she could improve by hard work, doing her best to overcome her faults. Dominic respected her for that. But if she fancied him, he didn't want to know. If Nicole Girard had thrown herself at him stark naked he seriously doubted he would respond, or even that he would be able to respond.

He was tortured through sleepless nights by the absence of Anna. Sometimes in restless dreams he could still feel the perfect ripeness of her weight in his arms when he lifted her. Most of all, he missed reaching out for her, tumbling round and round and up through heaven with her, in the night.

He rose and put out a hand, rested it lightly on Claude's shoulder.

'If you want Nicole,' he said, 'then go out and get her. You might try,' he added, more to himself, 'sending her flowers.'

Anna was laughing.

'No, no, *elbow* height,' she said. 'Like this.'

The carpenters had come to install the *barres* and mirrors in the studio.

It hadn't been hard to find the right kind of premises: the entire second storey of a house in the street behind Pendleton High Street. The ground floor was a hardware shop.

The room facing the road, which Anna supposed had been the master bedroom when the building was residential, ran the entire width of the house. It was large and light, ideal.

The other, smaller rooms could be used for storage; in one of them she could install an electric kettle and the paraphernalia for making snacks and coffee.

All for ten pounds a week.

'It's perfect,' she said to the owner, who also ran the shop. 'Except—won't you mind the constant thumping of a piano and the kids' noise?'

'Shouldn't expect so. Always did enjoy the patter of little feet.'

'Well . . . it can be more like a herd of elephants once they really get going.'

'Not to worry. I can always turn off my hearing aid, if it comes to that. And the rent'll come in handy.'

Her father found a piano for her, 'Though where I'm going to find somebody to play it for me, Lord only knows!' Anna said, hugging him when he told her.

Her words were mock-despairing, but Helen and Martin felt the mood behind them, a mood which for the first time in months was full of enthusiasm and hope.

In the event it was easy to find a pianist.

Perhaps the most exciting part of all the preparation was that Anna managed to master the first few simple steps of several *barre* routines herself.

When she found she could work in the centre again, doing some steps without support, she felt an exuberance she thought had left her forever.

She took it carefully, slowly; she began to find her limitations. And finding them to stay within them, accepting them.

When at last she was ready to advertise and open her doors for business she was overwhelmed. There were so many candidates for her four after-school classes for young beginners that she had to find words of polite refusal.

'I've got to keep the classes small, you see,' she said over and over again into the telephone. 'Perhaps your daughter can come along next term. I'm so sorry.'

The evening before she gave her first lesson Anna made a slow and careful tour of inspection in the studio, checking things, touching things. It was well-ordered, she decided, bare and austere as a serious studio should be, the way Régine Barrère's had been.

Suddenly Anna's hand flew to her mouth and she

clenched her eyes tightly shut against the memories which danced and spun behind them, forcing hot sobs to well up into her throat for the first time in days.

She mustn't allow herself to think of Barrère, of the joys of struggling for perfection in the days when she and Dominic had danced together for the first time. She must not.

Her studio was nothing like that. It was nothing more or less than a place where little girls would come after school; they would learn better posture and perhaps a few elementary steps of classical ballet. That was all.

Anna sighed and picked up her coat, turned out the studio lights, and made her way down the stairs, out of the shop, and home.

Her mother told him where to find her.

'But look, love, sit with me and have a cup of tea first. She won't be finished until five, and the children won't have left for ten or fifteen minutes after that. If—if you're to talk with her properly, you won't want competition from a bunch of little girls.'

Nor would it be pleasant for either of them if Anna refused to speak to him in front of her class. Neither Helen nor Dominic said that. There was no need.

'How is she?' he asked.

'Oh, she's well, really well. And so much happier now she's working. I don't suppose it seems very exciting after—' Helen bit her lip and turned away. 'I'll just put the kettle on, shall I? You sit down and make yourself comfortable.'

Dominic sat down, though he wasn't comfortable.

Helen was welcoming enough, warm, unmistakably pleased to see him again, though startled too, to find him on her doorstep in the winter sunlight without warning.

He had been about to ring her from London; he had debated with himself about doing that so long he nearly missed his train. In the end he decided it was better not to; it would only embarrass Helen to be forced to tell him not to come because Anna wouldn't see him.

Anna damned well would see him. He'd finally made up his mind about that. She would see him if he had to pursue her up the stairs to her bedroom and batter down the door.

He hated to put Helen and Martin on the spot, perhaps to create an unpleasant scene in a home where he'd been shown nothing but kindness, at least from them. But he was tired, thoroughly drained by the weary grind of non-stop work, so deadened by the strain of having a huge, gaping Anna-sized hole in his life that courtesy seemed very secondary.

God knows she'd made it plain enough she didn't want to know him. The letters he'd written were thrown carelessly into a kitchen drawer in his flat; she hadn't even opened them before she slung them back at him. He read them through again before he put them away.

And the phone calls. It had got to the point where he dreaded trying to ring her, feeling so damned awkward for Helen when she had to tell him yet again, with agonized compassion for him and what he must be feeling, that Anna wouldn't come to the telephone.

Never once did she insult him by offering a 'social' fiction, by saying that Anna was out when she wasn't, or holding out any hope that Anna would ring him back. She always asked how he was, really caring, really wanting to know. He was honest with her too. He always laughed a little, embarrassed, and said, 'I'm miserable without her, Helen.'

He held back news of his dancing, minimizing the deluge of invitations which were coming to him thick and fast, sure indications that his international career was becoming daily more assured, more solid. It might seem he was crowing, bragging, if he spoke of that.

Italy in the spring, and after that probably France again, and then possibly New York or even Tokyo.

Anyway, to speak of it would be to make it sound more exciting than it was. Without Anna by his side, without her love, it was just—living.

Anna would probably know about the invitations anyway from the trade journals. Unless it was really true that she no longer loved him, that she'd really meant it when she said she didn't care, that as she couldn't dance beside him there was nothing left for them. If she'd meant it, she wouldn't be likely to bother with following his progress through the *Dancing Times*.

Oh, but surely she hadn't really meant it! How could she have, after all they had been to one another? It was just that she had lost so very much. She'd needed time to get over that, time to readjust.

The whole thing boiled and raged in him until he hadn't been able to bear it any longer. He had to try to see her, to talk with her, to make her see reason—or else he would go mad.

The studio was accessible by an inside stairway leading from the shop. Helen also told him that the door at the bottom of the stairs wouldn't be locked by the time he got there. The shopkeeper greeted him cheerfully, and when he realized Dominic hadn't come to buy nails or a garden rake he said, 'Come to collect one of the little 'uns, eh?'

On the stairs Dominic felt suddenly queasy, and his palms were damp; he had to steady himself to avoid being knocked over by two little girls who clattered down past him, woollen mufflers flying, shrieking with giggles.

Then he was in the corridor. 'Turn left,' Helen had said, 'go straight along to the end.'

'Anna?'

'Dominic!'

Anna was standing by the piano, shuffling through some sheets of music; the studio lights had been turned off, and the curtains at the deep bay window thrown open. When she turned to face him she was outlined in daylight from behind, a graceful woman with spun-gold hair. He had forgotten how very beautiful she was.

Dominic stepped slowly into the room, and Anna moved too; for the space of a heartbeat it seemed as though she would move toward him, into his arms.

Instead she placed the music on its stand with precise care and cleared her throat.

'How did you know where to find me?'

'I went to your home first, and your mother told me you were here. This is really great, Anna, it's—'

'Small beer compared to the glamour of the London stage.' Her voice was flat.

'No, Anna, it isn't that at all! It's wonderful that you're well and working, and—'

'I suppose you planned this with my mother, to surprise me like this.'

'No, of course not. I didn't even ring first. I *had* to see you, to talk to you.'

'We've nothing to say to one another. Now you've seen that, you'd better go.'

'I came to tell you that I love you, Anna. I miss you so terribly.'

It was as though she hadn't heard him.

'Since you did come, it's a pity you weren't here a few minutes sooner. You could have given my little girls the very special treat of being able to watch a real dancer. They would have been thrilled. Most of them will never—'

'Anna, please don't.'

'I'm perfectly serious. Now if you'll excuse me, even a provincial ballet teacher has work to do.'

'Anna, why are you acting like this? You've sent my letters back, you won't even speak to me on the telephone. I've been frantic. Anna, why?'

'I've told you, Dominic, and now you can see for yourself. I have one life. You have another. There's no point—'

'There's every point!'

'What can an international star possibly have in common with a small town—'

'Oh stop it, Anna! That's not the way it is at all, and you know it.'

'It's the way it is for me.'

She turned away. Firmly and with finality she closed the lid of the piano as though to end the conversation.

He walked quickly to her side, caressed her shoulder, tried to turn her into his arms.

Anna stepped away from him and stood quite still, looking into his eyes. Her face was shadowed slightly and he couldn't read the expression there. But he had felt her trembling when he touched her; again there had been a split second when it seemed that she would soften.

She drew a deep breath and pressed the back of her hand across her lips until they had stopped trembling.

'Dominic, will you please just . . . go?'

He lingered a moment longer, and then without another word he nodded slightly, turned, and walked away.

Nicole was in when he rang her from King's Cross.

She listened to the rapid pips and wondered who might want to talk to her at quarter to eight on a Tuesday evening. She had been about to poach an egg and crawl into bed.

'Pizza? I'd like that. Will you give me half an hour?'

She wasn't tired any more, and she wasn't going to mess about playing hard to get.

Nicole felt terrible about what had happened to Anna. Hell, anybody half way human would, most especially a fellow dancer. They all felt terrible, and they missed her deeply.

A thing like that was hard, and it could happen to any one of them; it certainly wasn't something to gloat over.

The fact that Anna Farnell's illness and her incomplete recovery had given Nicole the opportunity every ambitious dancer dreams of made her feel worse about it than almost anyone else. She would never have wished a thing like that on Anna. As for the opportunity—well, opportunity could always be found if you were willing to work hard enough. You didn't need to build your career on somebody else's tragedy.

But it had happened, and since she'd been working with Dominic their partnership had been getting stronger all the time.

Everybody knew that Anna was out of Dominic's picture personally as well as professionally, that she had erased herself deliberately from his life, and that she didn't look likely to come back.

Dominic was pretty broken up about it, that was obvious. He had come back to London in a black and terrible mood, aloof from everything and everyone except when he was actually working. He was working as well as ever, better even, if that was possible.

He worked until he dropped, and then he disappeared until it was time to work again. No parties that anyone knew of, no social life at all. Just work, and more work.

If the ice man was about to thaw in her direction,

Nicole wasn't going to waste any time in getting on with it. She'd fancied him for months.

And after the pizza, 'Coffee?'

'Yes, thanks.'

That meant bed, everybody knew that. That was fine.

The first coffee-flavoured kiss was fantastic. Nicole hadn't all that much experience; the sum of what she had placed her firmly into the category of the non-promiscuous.

She was flirtatious when she went out with guys; when her dancing schedule allowed her the luxury of a late night she enjoyed parties and candle-lit dinners as much as any girl. But she was careful to keep most of her relationships with men light and breezy, casual, as she'd done with Claude.

But she had enough experience to realize she wanted Dominic in a way she'd never really wanted any other man.

He didn't disappoint her. He was gentle and urgent by turns, bringing her to a peak of ecstasy and then another and another until she lay sated and sleepy, fully satisfied.

Nicole slept then, though Dominic could not. He got out of bed and left the room, closing the door softly behind him.

He went into the sitting-room, turned on a lamp and threw himself into a chair; he picked up a book and stared at text he wasn't really taking in. When he realized he'd read the same sentence four or five times, he threw the book aside and began to pace the room.

Nicole had given herself eagerly. But it had meant nothing to him beyond the automatic response of any healthy, perfectly fit male animal to the intimate presence of a beautiful and desirable female.

Nicole was not Anna. Her embrace had left him . . . cold. Cold, and angry with himself that he had taken advantage of the girl's eager willingness to share his bed.

Dominic was awake to watch the dawn come up. When he heard Nicole stirring he brewed coffee and took it into the bedroom. He smiled wearily into her eyes as they drank it.

'You've been up all night,' she said gently.

'Yes.'

She stared down into the fragrant steam from her cup and nodded, waiting for him to go on.

'Nicole, I saw Anna yesterday, and I thought I could forget. I wasn't being fair to you. I'm sorry.'

She reached for his hand. 'Don't worry about it, okay?' she said. 'I think I understand, and it won't change anything between us at work, honestly not.'

They got dressed and went out into the grey, chilly London morning.

Dominic put her into a taxi and she sat back, sighing philosophically as the driver pulled away from the kerb.

Nobody can stay in love with a ghost forever, she told herself. In the meantime, she would see him every day, or nearly every day when he was in London. There would be other times . . .

CHAPTER SEVENTEEN

Anna stood at the window for a long time in the dusk. She watched the passers-by in the street below making their way back to the houses they had left that morning, looking forward to the tea and television of a late winter evening that was like any other.

Dominic in the doorway, watching her, reaching out to her, pleading with her. Dominic . . . saying he still loved her, still wanted her.

Dominic . . . more dear to her even than in the dreams which came unbidden, dreams of the past which wouldn't leave her. Dominic.

At last Anna drew the curtains and went back through the flat to get her coat and bag. She walked quickly down the stairs, stumbling a little; she locked the door at the bottom, and when the owner came through from the back of the shop she apologized for keeping him late.

She rang her mother from a call box near the post office.

'I'd thought of taking a walk, mum. Don't wait dinner for me, all right?'

'Anna?'

'Yes, mum?'

'Are you all right?'

Anna forced a rising note of cheer into her voice, tried to make her words sound firm, convincing.

'Of course I am, mum. I'm fine. I just want to be on my own for a bit.'

'Anna, I'm sorry if you were upset this afternoon. I didn't mean—'

'It's all right, mum, honestly.'

Anna meant the words to sound light, but they came into Helen's ear like hard little pellets of sleet.

Martin came home a few minutes later to find her slumped at the kitchen table, her head in her hands.

'What's up, love?'

'Martin, I didn't know what else to do for the best. He looked so hurt, so—'

'Hey, what the devil are you on about? Who looked hurt? What happened?'

'Dominic came to talk to Anna, and I told him where she was. She just rang. Says she wants to be on her own for a while, that we're not to wait dinner for her. I'm sure she was upset.'

'She must have sent Dominic away again.'

'She didn't say. I suppose she must have done.'

Martin whistled softly. 'Then that must be what she wants, or what she thinks she wants. In any case, I think you did the right thing.'

'But—'

'Helen, if she doesn't want him, then it's only fair she tells him to his face. She's got back on her feet a bit now, and I think it would be wrong if we tried to wrap her up in cotton wool.'

Helen nodded slowly, then looked up at him and smiled. 'I'm a softy,' she whispered.

'That you are and all, and I wouldn't have it any other way. Tell you what, let's have a sherry first and then I'll take you out for a steak.'

'I've cooked.'

Martin stood behind her chair, put his arms around her shoulders, and bent to kiss her soft cheek.

'I'll bet it will keep until tomorrow, love,' he said.

The night wind ruffled Anna's hair and made her eyes water as she dawdled on a slow, aimless circuit of the town; her coat collar was turned up and her hands were jammed in her pockets: she looked like a little girl who had lost her way, who was forced to wander up one road and down another until she recognized her home.

Dominic had touched her shoulder, and she had turned away; she had told him to go, and he had gone.

She had been abrupt with him, almost rude. He had stood there looking at her, his love for her naked in his dark eyes. What was it he had said?

Oh, what difference did it make!

She had said the only thing possible: they no longer had anything in common. He was an international dancing star, and she a provincial ballet teacher.

And her feelings for him?

Anna stopped walking and stood quite still, hunching down into her coat collar; the full force of her feelings for Dominic swept through her like a gust of strong wind. She shivered violently, and walked on. She loved him, loved him as much as she had from the beginning, but she had to try not to. And she had built a new life for herself apart from him, hadn't she?

Had she?

Anna turned into a road near her own; the soft glow of lamplight from behind the curtained windows spilled out, hinting at the lives being lived inside. Eating, or talking, or doing homework, or quarrelling or making love—whatever went to make up a life. Anna could almost envy them.

But I'm too young for that! Too young! I have danced in London, in Paris; I could have had the world. And love. And I lost it.

Anna quickened her pace, hurrying homeward. She had solved nothing, could solve nothing, but she had walked long enough, and she was tired.

She was grateful to find her parents out when she let herself in. She went to her room and gathered all the precious reminders of Dominic around her on her bed. She sat there far into the night, sifting through them. Remembering.

Most of the mothers who wheedled and begged or even tried to bribe their childrens' way into Anna's classes were of a type, confiding to her that although their small daughter—and occasionally small son—seemed no more or less amazing than any other boundlessly energetic child, she (or he) was destined for a brilliant stage career.

Anna couldn't understand it. Her own need to dance had come from within herself, a pure and joyous spring which her parents had managed to nourish without forcing. Helen had always encouraged her, and so had Martin. But they had never crossed the delicate line between 'encouragement' and 'pressure'.

'I would have danced myself,' Anna heard more than once. 'But you know how it is. Once I got married and the children started coming, well . . .'

There would be a sigh of gentle regret, a vague unspoken suggestion of some wonderful career which had been abandoned on the altar of marriage and family.

Anna was never so rude as to dispute any of these claims, though they irritated her. The women who made them were obviously trying to impress her; she doubted if any one of them could have tap-danced her way out of a paper bag.

Her father roared when she said that to him.

'They're usually the mothers with money to burn, right? People who live in Radleigh Cross or on one of the more prosperous-looking estates?'

'How did you know?'

'Oh, it's fairly simple, love. They've come from the city to live in the country. But when at all possible, they're determined to bring the bright lights with them in the boot of the expensive estate car. They've probably heard of you, Anna. And pride themselves in having a touch of culture.'

She grinned. 'You might be right.'

'What do you tell them?' he asked.

'Oh, just that I'm not trying to create ballerinas, but I do hope to teach the joy of music. With better posture and a sense of physical coordination as a bonus.'

'They won't want to hear that.'

'No. They'd like me to say that their child had talent.'

Theresa Anderson wasn't like that, she wasn't pushy; Anna could feel that, even when one of the first things Theresa said about seven-year-old Carmel was that she had talent. She rang Anna early in April, and when Carmel was refused because Anna's classes were full, she asked for a personal interview.

Theresa was slender and dark and soft-spoken, neat in her beige tailored suit; it crossed Anna's mind that she might have trained as a dancer herself.

'I'm sorry, Mrs Anderson, really I am. But if I take your daughter into one of my classes now she won't get the individual attention I feel each of the children deserves.'

'Couldn't she come sometimes just to watch the others?'

'It really would be better if you take her elsewhere,' Anna said politely. 'I've the names of two other teachers in the area. Both of them are qualified, and run larger classes . . .'

'Miss Farnell, I—' She hesitated, as though she wasn't sure how what she wanted to say would be received.

'I have seen you dance, in London,' she continued

finally. 'If you haven't room for Carmel, then I'd sooner not have her in ballet class at all.'

It came as a shock to Anna. It jolted her whole world to hear someone, a stranger, come out with it at last: 'I have seen you dance . . .'

Anna felt icy cold. She swallowed hard.

'Mrs Anderson, the other teachers are competent to guide your daughter's introduction to dance as well or better than I could, though perhaps they're not so well-known.'

'I didn't mean it that way,' Theresa said quickly, sensitive to Anna's tone. 'Really I didn't. I'm sure the other teachers are good. It's just that I know enough of classical ballet myself to realize how important the first training is, and to know you are the best. And to think Carmel may well have some real talent.'

There it was again. Carmel had real talent, and therefore if she had lessons with a dancer who had once been on the verge of international fame—no, that wasn't fair. She couldn't over-react forever, whenever she was reminded . . .

'At seven,' Anna said, 'your daughter is very young to be, well—' She searched for a word that would be tactful.

'She's too young to be pushed,' Theresa supplied, smiling. 'Yes, I know that. I know how that can go. It's awful to watch.' She laughed.

'Are you a dancer yourself?' Anna asked, relaxing, liking the woman and her directness.

'No I'm not, though I thought at one time I'd like to be.' She shrugged, still smiling. 'Quite frankly, I simply wasn't good enough.'

'That did it,' Anna said to her mother later. 'When Theresa Anderson didn't claim to be a genius who had sacrificed her all for home and family, I had to take Carmel.'

'Do you think she's talented?'

'I haven't met her yet, but I doubt it. Carmel is probably a chubby-cheeked, gap-toothed Charlie like all the rest of them. She'll be coming on Friday afternoons.'

'You're not trying to do too much?'

'Mum, I ask you! One little girl more or less? You know I'm happy as a lark.'

Helen knew she looked it, anyway. She had lost the hollow, haggard look of Christmas. She smiled more often, and said she was sleeping well.

If Anna ever thought of Dominic she never said so. In any case, since that confrontation in February his phone calls and letters and the nearly-constant barrage of flowers had stopped.

'There was no point in continuing the courtship,' Dominic said tiredly. 'She didn't—doesn't—want to know.'

'So you're quite free. To tour, I mean.' Steven Harwood riffled through the papers on the desk in front of him. 'They all want you, you know.'

'Yes,' Dominic said softly, 'I know. And yes, I'm quite free to tour anywhere in the world, dancing my heart out.' He stopped there and rose; he paced to the window of Steven's office and stood for a moment with his hands behind his back, looking down at the chaos of Covent Garden without really seeing it.

At last he turned and came back to Steven's desk and sat down again. 'I'm sorry, Steven. My personal life, or lack of it, shouldn't intrude in my work.'

'It hasn't, Dominic,' the older man assured him. 'If anything, I should say you're working far too hard, driving yourself.'

Dominic shrugged. 'What of it?'

Steven looked pained. He wouldn't pry, ever, and no one could ever accuse him of intruding in his dancers' private lives. But there had been something special about Anna and Dominic. Off-stage as well as on. And since they had parted so abruptly, after Anna's illness, Dominic Lautrec had changed from one of the happiest, most exuberant dancers Steven had ever known into an unhappy young man, rapidly hardening into a bitter man. Bitter. Yes, that was it.

It had nothing to do with the quality of his dancing.

No one who picked up the review section of a Sunday newspaper could miss the fact that Dominic's career was more than well-established; it had surpassed the wildest dreams of the most ambitious young dancer, and his fame was still spreading, his star still ascendant.

And there was more to it than just his genius for dancing, his power; Dominic Lautrec had 'charisma', they said. He was mentioned even in the cheaper tabloids, the papers without pretensions to an interest in serious ballet. There the grainy image of his handsome features could be seen in restaurants and airports, as he escorted this or that young woman from a television studio or a cinema. Usually the caption would enquire: 'Is it serious this time? Will it be marriage for the enigmatic superstar of Covent Garden?'

Steven wasn't fooled by any of that; he could remember the fragile beauty of Anna Farnell and her heart-stopping grace, the circle of light which had seemed to surround her and Dominic. He was deeply concerned; and so he dared to try to draw Dominic out, to see if there wasn't something he could do to bring them together again.

Anna must have seen at least some of the publicity, Steven thought; Anna must ache for Dominic, even as

Dominic ached for her. By rights Anna should have been beside him—if not dancing with him, then simply loving him.

Steven ached for both of them.

Anna predicted it, and she was right.

On Friday afternoon Theresa Anderson delivered her daughter to the studio at four sharp, presented Carmel to Anna, and promptly left the premises. She returned on the dot of five.

It was so much more usual for mothers to treat the sessions like social occasions of their own, lingering in the rear room of the flat where Anna kept the coffee things, helping themselves as though the fees they paid included refreshments.

'It's only an hour,' they would say. 'Hardly worth leaving and coming back.'

In some cases it seemed reasonable for them to feel that way. Some of Anna's pupils lived on estates in the furthest edges of Elmwood Centre, a fairly long way from Pendleton; most of their mothers used public transport because they didn't have cars.

It was never those mothers who stayed, or seldom. When they did, Anna didn't mind.

It was the ones Anna had come to think of as so pushy and aggressive who stayed. Even then she wouldn't have minded if they had come to watch the classes, but they didn't seem too interested. They stayed to gossip in her back room and drank her coffee.

Anna was glad to know that Theresa Anderson wasn't like that.

Nor was Carmel like any of the other children Anna taught. She recognized that on the first Friday.

All the children enjoyed performing the elementary steps Anna taught them. That was usual; it was what had always given Anna some measure of satisfaction in teaching them.

Carmel was a slender, graceful child; pretty, blonde, exceptionally musical. Carmel, fresh to the class, moved better than the others. Without knowing any steps, any of the basic positions, she seemed to dance from inside herself, with some innate knowledge of how to place her body and her legs and feet.

Carmel reminded Anna of what she had been like at that age. Even their temperaments were similar. When the lesson was finished Carmel came up to Anna with a shy smile, to thank her. And she asked if she could come to class every Friday afternoon.

CHAPTER EIGHTEEN

The month of June promised a rare gift: a perfect English summer. There was rain, but it was gentle, and it lasted only long enough to satisfy the farmers and gardeners. For the rest of the time it was hot and dry and sunny, with azure skies; there were whole strings of days like that, so many sparkling beads. The evenings were long, sweet-smelling with grass, mellow with light that seemed to last forever.

Elmwood Centre was thriving, and there were several newly-opened cafés along the river, very continental with huge striped umbrellas shading the tables on the terraces, dotted with the flower-coloured summer dresses of the girls who sat there with young men, talking, laughing.

Sometimes Anna walked along the river, and stopped at a café for coffee or a cold drink, but when she did that it seemed that the rest of the world was arranged in couples, two by two in the glorious summer weather, and it made her feel very much alone. But she wanted to be alone, when she wasn't actually working.

Early in June a young man who worked for her father asked her out to dinner. He was good-looking, he seemed nice enough, and he was genuinely sorry when Anna declined his invitation.

Anna had been busy since she began teaching. After Carmel came, she was so totally absorbed in her work that she felt that nothing else mattered to her. Not even her parents' tentative, gentle urgings had any effect: 'You're young and pretty, love; you ought to go out more, meet more people.'

Anna would smile gravely at that, and shake her head, and at last they stopped. Their daughter was working, she seemed happier; they would let it go at that.

'How's your budding ballerina coming along?' her father asked one evening.

'Which one?' Anna made a wry face at him.

'Carmel Anderson, of course,' he supplied, laughing. 'The only one you ever talk about.'

'Not fair! I talk about the others too. They're all making progress, each in her own sweet way. But—Carmel really *is* talented. It shines out of her. She's a joy to watch.'

'So you keep telling us. You're going to miss her during the break.'

'What break?'

'Summer hols, of course.'

'Um. I'm offering summer classes. No one else does, and there is a demand. Four classes each week as usual, plus Carmel's private lessons.'

'She's only seven,' Martin protested uneasily. 'Surely a bit young for—'

'Oh no, not at all! It's a treat for both of us.'

Anna still kept her classes deliberately small. She hadn't space in the studio for more than nine children in each session, ten or eleven at a stretch. She was convinced that even if she had, more would be too many. She was offering proper training to the children; she knew that, and she was proud of it.

Anna hoped to offer a great deal more than that to Carmel Anderson. She didn't speak of it like that, not then or later; Anna wasn't at all sure she could put what she meant into words, or that anyone would understand her if she tried.

But her eyes shone as she thought of it, of all she could teach Carmel.

With each child she taught, no matter how inept or awkward the child might be, Anna encouraged a good posture, a correct stance, from the very first lesson.

'Stand up straight with heads erect and shoulders down. No slumping, sagging, or bulging,' she insisted gently, over and over again.

That was the first lesson, often more easily taught than mastered, but Anna was patient. She was prepared to make the necessary corrections until at last it became a habit, or until she was sure each child understood what had been asked of her, and was trying hard to make it one.

Having got that far, Anna demonstrated the five basic positions of the feet with which nearly all the steps in classical ballet begin and end, and the correct positions of the arms to go with them.

She encouraged the children to master these elementary positions. But it was a variable achievement from one child to another, especially when Anna began, very slowly, to introduce the idea that each position must ultimately be learned with the whole leg turned outward from the hip joint.

Anna kept the whole thing very simple and relaxed. Knowing she mustn't demand too much, or make it seem like all work and no joy, she reserved a part of each class just for the exuberant romp in which the children were free to dance as they liked.

She planned to offer intermediate classes later, as the keenest children showed a desire to learn more, or as older children with some previous training came to join. Even then she knew that there could never be a straight progression from beginner to intermediate, that the rate of progress within each class would always be a highly individual matter.

Carmel Anderson joined the Friday class in April. In May, Anna approached Theresa and asked that her daughter be allowed to come on Saturday mornings as well.

'I'd like the chance to work with her alone,' Anna said. 'She's streets ahead of the others, and interested enough to be able to concentrate for longer periods of time. There's no question of your paying an extra fee, of course.'

'I certainly wouldn't expect you to devote your time to her as a gift.'

Anna laughed. 'I really wouldn't mind. Oh, and this summer I could give her more time in the week as well, whichever day would suit best.'

'We're off to Dorset for a week in July, but for the rest of the time we'll be here. She'd love it. It's the only thing she talks about.'

So it was settled, for Saturdays and summer Wednesday mornings.

Working with Carmel gave Anna's life a focus; at last she could feel she might really achieve something by her teaching, a pupil she could point to with pride.

When the image of Dominic's face, the sound of his voice, the clear memory of his touch came back in dreams to haunt her, she pushed the spectres down. As relentlessly she drove them from her waking thoughts so they couldn't dominate her days. *She had Carmel to teach.*

Anna saw Dominic in newspapers often, or rather she saw his newsprint ghost. She read all the accounts of his brilliant success. She read that he had been offered a film, a television spectacular, seasons of his own throughout the world.

She was wistfully pleased for him, though she ached

to remember how close she had come to sharing the fame, the excitement of it with him.

But the gossip of his private life, pairing him off accurately or not with one woman after another, tore through her and left her shaking, sometimes with tears of hot, angry jealousy pouring down her face. The strength of that feeling shocked her; she tried very hard to fight it. What was it to her that Dominic . . .

Anna tried to wrench the tangled roots of her love for him out of her mind and soul and body so she would be at peace. She couldn't. When the effort became too great, she went off by herself for a while and held her burning face in trembling hands until she regained some self-control.

And she continued to read of him in newspapers, trade journals, dancing magazines. She couldn't seem to stop; she wasn't even very sure she wanted to.

After Carmel came to her, though, there were days when their sessions together were so satisfyingly rich, so full of joy, that Anna could get through them almost peacefully.

'You're very supple,' Anna said. 'That's good, It's very good. It means you'll be able to manage the full degree of turn-out from your hips, and *without* letting your bottom stick out at all.'

Carmel giggled shyly. 'Sometimes it does, though.'

'Ah, *now* perhaps. But little by little you'll develop more strength in your muscles, and it will become easier—so natural and right you'll be able to do it without thinking about it.'

Carmel's back and heels were flat against the wall. When she bent her knees above the toes of her turned-out feet, allowing the shoulders and back to slide gently down the wall as she'd been asked to do, it was easy for

Anna to see that the child was lithe as a cat.

'If I work very hard, I'll be able to do *everything* that much more quickly.'

Carmel's tone was matter-of-fact, but her eyes were shining with pride and determination and happiness.

'Yes, Carmel, that's right. Little by little, you'll be able to do everything.'

Long before the end of the summer Anna was sure of that. Carmel listened and worked with quiet, concentrated, patient dedication. Her sessions with Anna were about more than learning stance, position and steps; more than intermediate exercises at the *barre* or simple *enchainements* of steps in the centre of the studio floor. Having the gifted child to teach inspired Anna to stretch herself to the limits of her strength and skill to convey the beauty and freedom at the very core of dance itself.

Occasionally, Anna's intensity reached a pitch at which she was frustrated and angry because she couldn't demonstrate a step she wanted Carmel to see, to appreciate.

Oh, but not to try by herself. Not yet; Carmel was far too young. One does not force a child, no matter how gifted. One must not!

Then Anna would be reminded so painfully of her own weakened body that she came very near to despair.

There was one terrible morning, brilliant with motes of August sunlight dancing, mocking her, across the wooden floor, when she tried to show Carmel an *arabesque*.

Anna found her *pointe* slippers, tied the ribbons, showing Carmel with care how that was done. Then, poised in the centre of the studio, she rose to *demi-pointe*, and then to full *pointe*, on her right foot.

She knew the sequence. Christ, she ought to know it; she'd danced it often enough. From demi-pointe *to full-*

pointe *on her right foot, with her left leg extended behind her in the longest line possible from fingers to toes*.

She couldn't manage it. Her right foot came down hard, flat, onto the floor.

Everything flooded back: the years and years of work, the brief glory, the terrible pain of losing Jason and the raw, dripping day of his funeral, the bewilderment and grief, the long struggle to come to terms with a body which no longer obeyed her automatically. Sending Dominic away, back to his career, so he could . . . soar . . . without her.

That was a kind of sequence too, and it had taken everything away from her.

Anna turned her head away, and put the back of her hand quickly to her mouth to try to stifle the choking sob she couldn't check; it sounded like a hiccup, and she managed a smile.

'Oh Carmel, it's far too warm to dance *sur les pointes*!' she said. 'Besides, you won't be dancing on your *pointes* for years yet. That's very, very important, you know— not to begin before you're ready. For now we shall concentrate on *barre* work, okay?'

Anna talked about her progress with her classes while James examined her, pausing only while he checked her blood pressure and her pulse. When he finished he stood by the examining table and blew out his cheeks, regarding her.

'You're fine, Anna. But don't you feel you're concentrating unduly on this Anderson child . . . Carmel?'

'What makes you say that?'

'It sounds as though you're pushing her. As though you're obsessed with her, obsessed with every new step she learns, each new—'

'That's ridiculous!' Anna looked perplexed. 'You

asked me to tell you how I'm doing and I told you. I'm teaching an outstandingly talented child. What do you expect me to do? Restrict her to baby lessons?'

'She *is* a baby, Anna, in balletic terms at least.'

'Oh, what can you possibly know?'

James was seldom angry, seldom even impatient with Anna. Now he saw, or thought he saw, that Carmel had come to represent for her everything she herself had lost, everything she might have achieved if it hadn't been for the awful blow of losing her own performing career just at the point where the whole world seemed hers for the taking: fame, money . . . love.

'Perhaps you see your younger self in her,' he said.

Anna sat up and pushed herself off the table.

'I came here for my routine examination. Now it's finished, I think I'd better be getting home. I'm tired, and I've a lot of work to do.'

'Anna, please listen to me.'

'You can't have it both ways, James. I have a new life now, a life you pleaded with me to build for myself. I've got a kind of purpose. Teaching Carmel is part of it. She gives me the inspiration to teach all the others, the kids who'll never remember ballet lessons as anything more than something they did once a week for an hour after school.'

'Yes, yes, I know all that, but—'

'Do you?' Her eyes were hard on his, challenging.

'I think so, Anna. I believe you when you say Carmel is talented. I trust you to know the difference, believe me I do. I know how important she is to you. But you must not push her.' He said the last words quietly, separating them for emphasis.

Anna spoke quietly too. 'You must try not to put me down.'

'Anna, the child simply isn't ready for the things you're trying to teach her. How old is she? Six?'

'Seven.'

'Well, then—'

'You sound as though I'm trying to put her into toe shoes!'

'No, of course not that. But she's growing, Anna; I do know that. Her muscles and ligaments and tendons must not be stretched beyond their own easy limit.'

Anna began to speak, but he interrupted her.

'Her concentration mustn't be channelled too narrowly either. You say she loves to dance, and I believe that as well. But she's only seven years old, for God's sake!'

Anna turned away and clenched her hands. 'I was five when I started classes . . .'

'I'm sure you were. But how far did your teacher attempt to take you before you auditioned for White Lodge when you were ten?'

She turned back to him, her face as still and set as an engraving.

'She took me exactly as far as her own knowledge, and my—talent—allowed us to go. Goodbye, James.'

CHAPTER NINETEEN

It was November. The trees were leafless and the earth bare, asleep beneath a crust of frost.

Inside the warm studio it could have been any season. The morning light streamed in at the window and danced on the walls.

'I wish it was summertime,' Carmel said wistfully,

Anna laughed. 'We all do, love. The only thing that makes winter bearable is having Christmas to look forward to. It's cold and wet and rainy most of the time.'

'I don't mind that so much. It's school I don't like.'

'But Carmel, I thought you did!'

'It's boring. Even when it's not meant to be. When our lessons are over, we're supposed to be making paper chains for our school's Christmas tree. Or practising the play. I'm to be a snowflake this year.'

'Not a very cheerful one, by the sound of it.'

Carmel shrugged. 'It's babyish. I like coming here much better, and in summertime I came twice a week by myself, *and* once with the others. I was *really* making progress then.'

'You're still making progress, Carmel. And school's important too, you know.'

'But all I want to do is be a dancer. I don't need school for that.'

'Of course you do. Even dancers need to know languages and maths and geography—all the things you'll learn at school. Why, even if you go to a special dancing school you'll have classroom lessons every day.'

'Um, but I'd have dancing lessons every day too, wouldn't I?'

'Yes, but at first only for an hour or so. Anyway, you won't be old enough to get into a dancers' boarding school for years yet. Not until you're ten or eleven.'

'I wish I would hurry up and get older.'

Anna smiled, hearing that.

She was increasingly excited about Carmel's progress. The child would almost certainly be accepted by a professional ballet school when she was old enough to audition. Unless she lost interest somewhere along the line, or unless adolescence made her gawky or overly-tall for the dancing stage, Carmel would achieve her ambition to be a dancer, Anna felt sure.

'Meanwhile, let us learn what we can, shall we?'

Carmel grinned as she took up her position at the *barre*.

Anna guided her through a warm-up, and then through the exercises and *enchainements* which formed the base of their Saturday morning lesson.

In the months since they had begun working privately together, the routine had changed very little. What had changed was Carmel's ease and confidence in getting through it, and the complexity of the *enchainements* of steps she was able to perform in the centre of the studio.

Her memory was astonishingly good, and her capacity for learning more and still more seemed limitless.

Anna had only to correct a fault once for Carmel to understand what was wrong with the line of leg or foot or spine. Or her stance as she assumed a basic position. Or the carriage of her arms.

The mutual sympathy between the two—Anna's fierce desire to teach Carmel everything she could, and

Carmel's corresponding eagerness to learn, made the hour-long session on Saturday morning seem far too brief.

In the autumn, when Carmel returned to school, Anna hit upon the idea of stretching the lesson.

'Not to include more actual dancing,' Anna said to Theresa Anderson. 'Simply half an hour or so at the end of it, a bit of time in which we can talk. We can talk about the history of ballet, and mime, and stage make-up, and—oh, so many things.'

Carmel loved that too. Above all, she seemed to enjoy poring over Anna's collection of dance magazines. Anna brought them out for Carmel to see, as well as for very different reasons of her own.

As she analyzed one after another of the photographs of dancers she had known and worked with, pointing them out to Carmel, Anna hoped that the tight ring of pain and bitterness around her heart would ease little by little, and that in time she could look at the pictures without her pulse racing wildly at the injustice of the fact that her own was not among them.

Anna tested another of her own reactions when she carefully selected a magazine in which Dominic's photograph appeared several times: alone, with Nicole Girard as his partner, and again with the entire Company in a recent production of *Swan Lake*.

'Ooh, the Swan Queen is lovely,' Carmel said, her eyes saucer-round. 'The Prince is handsome too. Just as a Prince should be.'

'Yes, just—just as he should be,' Anna faltered. 'That's Dominic Lautrec. He's one of the finest male dancers alive today. One of the youngest as well.'

She nearly poured it all out. She nearly blurted out her own tragic story, the tale of how she herself had come within a hair's breadth of comparable fame, by his side. But she knew that she must never burden Carmel with the grim details of what she had come through to be teaching elementary ballet in Pendleton.

When Carmel was older she might guess it, or part of it; if she continued to study ballet she would almost certainly come across an old photograph of Anna Farnell somewhere or other.

Anna's hand shook slightly as she folded the magazine closed and set it aside.

It's still too soon. I should have known better than to drag out Dominic's picture! Good God, I can't risk breaking down again in front of the child! The fiasco last summer was bad enough.

Anna forced a calm smile. 'Mr Lautrec is every bit as good at dancing his roles as he is good-looking,' she said matter-of-factly. 'And you'll be good enough to dance the Swan Queen one day, if you're patient, and if you want to badly enough.'

'I want it more than anything in the world.'

Carmel looked and sounded much older than seven when she said that.

On Friday afternoon Theresa sent Carmel outside to wait in the car while she had a word with Anna. Carmel hung back, glaring at her mother with a look of mutinous hurt which bewildered Anna when she saw it; Carmel was such a willing child. Anna couldn't think why she didn't obey immediately.

Theresa spoke sharply to her daughter; finally, reluctantly, without looking at Anna or speaking to her, Carmel snatched up her coat and scarf and stormed off down the stairs, slamming the door at the bottom.

Theresa said, 'I didn't want to tell you this over the telephone, Miss Farnell. Carmel won't be coming to you again for private lessons, not—for a while. She'll still come on Fridays for class, but—'

Anna was stunned into objecting. 'But *why*? She's doing so well, learning so very quickly. Oh, Mrs Anderson, if it's the extra money—'

Theresa was holding her car keys so tightly the metal teeth bit into her palm. She shoved them into her coat pocket.

'It isn't that. Nor is it any reflection on the superb quality of your work with her.'

'Then . . . what?'

'Carmel has become . . . obsessed with dancing, Miss Farnell, absorbed in it so totally that everything else in her life comes a very poor second. She's been so listless and apathetic at school her teacher felt obliged to speak to me about it. I'm sorry.'

Anna felt bowed down, exhausted by the weight of it. Obsessed. James had used that word too.

'Please don't blame yourself, Miss Farnell. It's at least as much my fault as anyone else's. I know my little girl, or at least I think I do. I should have seen this coming. I should have realized how single-minded she can be when the mood takes her.

'I have to admit I didn't. But her teacher told me she doesn't even play with the other children as she used to do, that she's not even remotely interested in the Christmas pageant coming up. Something has to give, you see.'

Anna nodded. 'I understand. I'm sorry for my part in this, but I really do understand. I'll do my very best to make the lessons less intense.'

They smiled at one another, tense, each equally desperate to find a word of comfort, to end the interview on a note of mutual forgiveness. They liked one another instinctively; in other circumstances they might have become close friends.

Afterwards Anna repeated the conversation over to herself in her mind. She edited it, rationalizing the worst of the guilt she felt until she managed to blur its edges. She was cheerful again by the time she got home. Carmel would still be coming to her classes every Friday afternoon.

When Theresa Anderson rang a week later, on Thursday evening, she sounded as if she had a cold, or as though she'd been crying.

'Miss Farnell, Carmel won't be at ballet class tomorrow. She sprained some ligaments in her knee.'

Anna gripped the receiver. 'What happened?'

'We had a full-scale family row over her dancing lessons. Carmel locked herself into the bathroom and refused to come out. When we heard her screaming, my husband managed to get to her by removing the door from its hinges. She had stuffed cardboard into her ballet slippers so she could dance on her toes.'

'No!'

Theresa sighed. 'I'm afraid so. She said she was trying to practise an *arabesque sur les pointes*, of all things.'

Anna caught her breath.

The August morning, the hot studio, the sequence she had tried to perform for Carmel, for ... herself. The miserable, painful failure.

Theresa continued speaking; Anna heard her dully, through a daze.

'She's not badly injured, and it certainly won't be permanent. She'll hobble around for a bit, but she'll be all right. And we know it's not your fault.

'We do have to help Carmel to try very hard to get everything back into perspective, of course, and for the moment we feel that must mean the end of ballet lessons altogether.

'Her father and I have promised her that when she's a few years older she can try for a stage boarding school.

Until then, Carmel and I will practise dancing together for an hour each week...'

'Yes, I see...'

'Miss Farnell, Carmel keeps telling me that you warned her many times not to do anything so foolish as dancing on her toes, and I know it's true.'

It was true, but Anna found it very little consolation.

CHAPTER TWENTY

'Anna, what a pleasure it is to see you.' James's smile spread slowly across his face and reached his eyes.

The night wind was sharp, cold. Anna could feel it through her long coat and leather boots. She shivered slightly and jammed one gloved fist into her pocket.

'I came to say you were right about Carmel. I'm sorry. I really am.'

She turned abruptly and started back down the three stone steps to the street.

'Anna, come back!'

She stopped on the last step and looked back over her shoulder.

'Please have a drink with me, Anna. I've had one hell of a rotten day, and it's so good to see a friend.'

'Truce?'

He laughed.

'I don't deserve it.'

'Come on in.'

Anna shrugged tiredly and came back up the steps, allowing James to escort her into the house and up the inside stairs into his flat.

James poured drinks and handed her one. 'What's up, Anna?'

She sipped and shook her head, sending her blonde hair tumbling around her shoulders; she looked away from him, and her hair hid her expression like a veil.

'I told you already. I came to say I'm sorry. You were right about Carmel.'

'Oh, you mean just because she sprained a few ligaments? That wasn't your fault.'

Anna looked at him directly; he could see the tears which glistened in the lovely smoky-grey eyes, the slightly quivering chin at the point of her delicate, heart-shaped face. He wanted to reach out and enfold her, to protect her.

'It was my fault,' she whispered. 'But how did you find out about Carmel?'

'I saw a note of her attendance in Outpatients when I went up to the hospital this afternoon. It wasn't serious, and it wasn't anything to do with you. Apparently she got herself tangled up in her skipping rope.'

'Is that what her parents said?'

'Well yes, I suppose they must have. That's what the registrar filled in for the cause of the accident. Why?'

Anna moved restlessly round the room, holding her drink in one hand, clenching and unclenching the other.

'Carmel's mother rang me this evening to say she won't be bringing her to ballet lessons any more. Which is just as well, because I won't be teaching—'

'Anna, would you care to stop wearing out my carpet? Please sit down and tell me what you're talking about.'

'I wasn't going to burden you with my problems.'

'That's what I'm here for, Anna.'

'That's just it! Your whole life's been devoted to cleaning up the messes other people make, including mine. I'm sick of myself, sick of the mess I've made of my life, sick of being bailed out time after time, sick of fooling myself. Just—plain—sick.'

She looked so defeated, saying that, so slight and graceful and so utterly lovely that again James wanted to go to her, to take her into his arms like any ordinary man. She was right about his life; he hadn't any problems of his own. He had spent years aloof, being doctor, playing God. She couldn't know the emptiness it left, always giving and refusing to take.

He said, 'Tell me about it, Anna. I promise not to prescribe anything but Scotch. Sometimes I'm sick of playing doctor, did you know that?'

Anna sat down and positioned her drink very carefully on the wide arm of the chair. She ran her index finger around the rim of the glass and stared at it. Then she recited what Theresa Anderson had told her as though she was reading from a script, and she told James why she was responsible for what Carmel had done.

'I can't dance. I can't love. I've even failed my great mission as a big fish in a little pond. I can't even teach elementary ballet to eager little girls.'

'Of course you can! There are others, Anna. You can still teach them. Why, they're queueing up to get into your classes.'

She sighed. 'Yes, but what's the point? I may as well take out a childminder's licence and open up a crèche. First position,' she mimicked. 'That's right, children! Now the arms, a graceful circle in the air. Lightly, lightly, children. There, that's fine.'

'It gives them pleasure, Anna. It teaches them a lot.'

'They can learn it anywhere. They don't need *me* to teach them. You were right, James. When Carmel came, I felt it was all worthwhile—as though at last I'd found someone who might be able to absorb everything I could give her.

'I forgot that she was far too young. I wanted her to carry all the burden of my own defeat, my own refusal to let go of what . . . might have been. You called it an obsession. Funnily enough, Carmel's mother used the same word. Isn't that funny?'

'No, Anna. Not very . . .'

The urge to cross the room, to take her into his arms and hold her, to soothe and shelter her, became stronger. He could just . . . reach out, and hold her.

Beautiful Anna. All the times when he might have reached out, touched her, offered her his love as an ordinary man. He could give her peace, a place, a kind of fulfilment. No. It wouldn't be enough, not really. She was born to fly; she deserved to fly.

He crossed to her to pour another drink.

'You know, James,' she said wistfully, looking up at him, 'sometimes I feel as though I was cursed from the very beginning. The fates or the gods or whatever allowed me to believe I was going to lead a charmed life, and just as I nearly made it they took a swipe and dashed me against the rocks. Nothing is left now.'

He poured the drink for her and went to sit down opposite.

'What are you going to do now?' he asked quietly.

Anna meant to shrug, but she found herself sobbing uncontrollably. 'I don't know. I—just—don't—know. I don't really feel like doing . . . anything at all . . . What shall I do, James?' The lovely eyes were wet and the slender hand shook as Anna raised her glass to sip from it. 'Where can I go, now that nothing is left?'

James took a breath. 'Go to Dominic, Anna. Take your chances.'

She shook her head. 'It's far too late for that. He's in New York just now anyway, rehearsing for the Christmas season. And for the first time, Nicole Girard was invited to appear abroad with him. They're a partnership now. I'm happy for them, glad for them.'

'You know all that?'

She nodded. 'I know. I still read the magazines, the trade papers. I can't seem to give it up.'

'No. But Anna, just because they've formed a stage partnership doesn't mean—'

'I know that too, but if they have I wouldn't blame them. I have nothing left to offer him, James.'

'You can love him, Anna.'

She bowed her head, anguished, and again the smooth veil of golden hair swung down to hide her features. 'I sent him away. I'm sure he's accepted that by now.'

'Perhaps so, but I feel—'

He stopped. He had played God long enough.

'You feel . . .'

She was looking at him eagerly.

'I feel you've tried to build a new life with your teeth clenched and your heart elsewhere. I feel it's time for you to take your chances with what's most important. That's what living, *really* living, is all about.'

'Yes,' she whispered, 'but how could I go?'

James grinned at her. 'Ever heard of Sir Freddie Laker?'

'At Christmas—'

'Ah, Christmas! Satsumas and walnuts and stockings filled with little surprises.'

'Yes. What about my parents?'

'They have each other, Anna.'

'They don't have Jason.'

'No, they don't. But they do have each other. It might surprise you, how much comfort they find in that. Go to Dominic, Anna.'

She looked up, past him, at some private vision of her own. Her eyes were shining and in the soft lamplight her hair made a kind of halo around the exquisite features of her face. 'I'll go to New York,' she said softly. 'I need to get away, and I need to . . . to watch him dancing . . .'

Presently Anna came out of her reverie and smiled at James. 'Oh yes, I'll go to New York!'

Anna sat on her bed, leafing idly through a months-old issue of *Dancing Times*.

She had looked at it so often the magazine opened automatically to the page she sought, and there they were: Dominic and Nicole, smiling for the camera, honoured to be invited to do a Christmas season in America.

They would be dancing Prokofiev's *Romeo and Juliet*, and other works, in New York.

Anna stared at the photograph one last time, wondering if their partnership had gone beyond the professional. Oh, but she had no right to wonder about that. Not any more. She had forfeited that right a long time ago—nearly a year ago. A lot could happen in a year.

She smoothed the magazine closed and put it away with the others: all the chronicles of Dominic's career since she had sent him away.

She wanted to watch him dancing, to see him triumphant, soaring, one last time. If she could do that, she might be able to get him completely out of her system, especially to watch him partnering Nicole.

Anna struggled with a thought, half-formed in her mind. Finally it came clear: she wanted to say goodbye to Dominic in her heart and to keep with her always the clear, strong memory of Dominic in flight, superbly victorious. Yes, that was it.

As for Christmas, that didn't mean so much to her now. It wouldn't really matter if she spent the day itself away from home, away from her parents. Nor even that she would spend it alone in a foreign country. She would miss the worst of it, the heart-tearing reminders that Jason wasn't there, that her parents were sad, aging, that life had very nearly robbed them of laughter.

Anna began to feel a bittersweet excitement at the prospect of what she was about to do.

Oh, but tickets! Tickets for the ballets! There wasn't much time, they might be sold out. She laughed suddenly in relief, running down the stairs to the telephone. Steven Harwood could get tickets for her if anybody could.

He was glad to do that, he said. If he was perplexed that Anna wanted to see as many performances as possible, especially of *Romeo and Juliet*, he covered it very well.

'Steven,' Anna said, 'please don't tell any of the others about my plans to be in New York.'

'No Anna, of course not.'

'It's just something I feel I have to do. It's silly, I suppose, but—'

'Not at all, Anna. Please don't worry. Enjoy New York, my dear. Oh, and if you should decide to be in touch with Dominic or Nicole while you're there, they're booked into the Chalfont. It's virtually within shouting distance of Times Square.'

Dear Steven! So tactful and so perceptive, as always.

He knew instinctively that she would either want very much to see Dominic, or that she would want to avoid him at all costs. Either way, he wanted to make it easy for her. What more practical way to do that than to tell her the name and location of his hotel? Steven knew, of course, that she would rather die than ask him for it.

'I think it's nice you'll get away for a bit, have a little break,' Helen said. 'Your dad and I aren't planning much of a fuss over Christmas this year. Maybe a meal in a restaurant on the day, nothing elaborate.'

The carollers were out again. The lights were up along the High Street and the Co-op well stocked with crackers and mince pies and frozen turkeys. Such seasonal reminders that had been actively painful for Helen the previous year now merely saddened her, made her aware that she was growing old.

Neither Helen nor Martin minded that Anna

wouldn't be with them for the holiday. If they knew why she was going to New York, they didn't say.

They cared for her, of course; they wanted more than anything to see her happy and settled. But they were wise, and they were reconciled to the truth that Anna would have to find her own way, in her own time.

CHAPTER TWENTY-ONE

She stood on the balcony outside her hotel room, dressed in Juliet's clinging, flowing robes.

The street below had been moved, and a garden had been set up in its place. Dominic was there, Romeo, holding out a single blood-red rose to her.

They mimed their love for one another, and the applause was deafening.

The curtain came down because it was the end of Act I, and then all the others were with them, and they were caught up in the usual back-stage chaos of the first interval.

The warning bell sounded for Act II...

The telephone rang. Anna fumbled sleepily for the receiver on the table by the bed, unwilling to leave the dream. It vanished before she could capture it. She opened her eyes and remembered where she was.

It was the desk clerk with her wake-up call, to allow herself time to dress and to eat something before she made her way to the theatre where Dominic and Nicole were dancing. Again.

After six days and five nights in New York, Anna was badly disorientated. Day and night seemed to run into one another, back to front; she was unable to sleep at night or stay awake during much of the day.

She had pictured herself as a conscientious tourist wearing sensible walking shoes, seeing the landmarks and museums of New York when she wasn't at the ballet. In the event, all of her energy was centred on seeing Dominic. On watching Dominic dance.

She had seen two performances of *Romeo and Juliet*, and one each of *Plastic Flowers* and *Doom*. She watched them hungrily, her heart thumping wildly in her breast, longing to touch him, to be in his arms. She closed her eyes and breathed slowly, deeply, every time the urge to rush to the stage came over her. *She couldn't do that. She couldn't! She had come to say goodbye to him, in her heart. There were more performances to come, and she would be there in the audience.*

Her tickets were good ones. Steven had seen to that. Anna sat in the very centre of the magnificent modern theatre, close enough to the stage to be able to see each gesture, every step. Evening after evening she withdrew yet another cardboard square from the zippered compartment of her handbag and gave it to the same, bored, gum-chewing usher, who never once looked up or spoke to her.

The city overwhelmed her at first. It was huge, crowded, dazzling, noisy. Even in the insulated comfort of her hotel room Anna could hear the roar of traffic in the street below.

But after the first day, Anna's New York became as familiar and as simply navigated as Pendleton. Her hotel was precisely four blocks from Dominic's, and that was a further ten blocks from the theatre in which he danced, and that was all that mattered.

In between there was non-stop, bustling humanity, and buildings so tall she couldn't see their topmost storeys without bending backwards at an almost impossible angle. Always, everywhere, there was noise.

Anna very quickly accepted the fact that she was one of thousands of people hurrying along restricted, private paths within the vastness of the place, a cipher with her own routine. She found that comforting.

She hadn't thought about walking to Dominic's hotel the first time she did so; when she came to it she stood in the doorway of an Italian restaurant opposite and stared at The Chalfont's entrance for a very long time.

That was just after dawn on her second day; she had spent a sleepless night pacing her hotel room following *Romeo and Juliet*. She knew she shouldn't walk alone through menacing night streets, but when light came at last she went out, hoping to tire herself enough to be able to sleep.

That became the pattern of her days and nights: in the evening, the ballet; afterwards the terrible effort to think about what she had seen, to bring her feelings out into the open and to accept and absorb them; a sleepless night. At first light, a walk. Then sleep, and then the theatre again.

Christmas Day might have come and gone unnoticed, had it not been for the fact that there was no performance of the ballet that evening. She spent the day alone, reading and walking, not really minding the solitude. In spite of the piercing cold and the lavish evidence of the season in every store window and the bigger than life lighted tree in the middle of Times Square it didn't feel like Christmas to her at all.

After nine days like that, while she was out walking one morning, Anna glanced through the plate-glass window of a restaurant as she passed it, considering whether or not she would go in for a cup of coffee.

Dominic was sitting at a table near the door, facing the street, warming his hands over a steaming cup. He glanced up just as she saw him, or thought she did; then she was sure. For one awful moment it seemed as though he was looking directly into her eyes.

Anna stared at him, open-mouthed; for the fraction of a second she couldn't move. Then she ran as quickly as she could, back in the direction of her hotel.

She was out of breath when she got there. It was only when she reached the safety of her room that she realized there were tears streaming down her face.

'I'm not going to the party. I'm going back to the hotel, to sleep as long as I possibly can. I'm sorry, but I'm dog tired.'

'Tell me about it, Dominic. It's not as though you're dancing all by yourself, you know. Look, they're laying on turkey and all the trimmings in our hon—'

'Nicole, please. Go. Eat. Enjoy yourself. As far as I am concerned, Christmas was cancelled this year due to lack of interest. Besides it was three days ago, and I don't like turkey. I'm sorry to be so unfestive, but all I really want is a meatball sandwich and a long nap, all right?'

The tiredness was familiar, but this trip had turned out to be more gruelling than most. This time the idiots seemed to feel that one hell of a lot of ballyhoo was included with the dancing in his contract.

The press was getting high on its own importance. The newspapers were bad enough, but the television boyos were much, much worse.

Worst of all were the endless 'chat' shows. *Yah-ta-ta, yah-ta-ta, yah-ta-ta*, until they were blue in the face.

Yes it was true he had been born in France, yes he considered London his permanent home, and incredibly, once, some overweight bitch with her gnarled, be-ringed hands all over his thigh had asked him on a live broadcast if he was queer.

She was the one who invited him to bed after the show.

He was a dancer, he kept telling them, a performing artist. What they saw on stage was what they got. But they wanted more. They kept coming at him, squeezing him until he thought he couldn't take it any more. He kept taking it. What the hell did it matter?

He kept smiling, raising one now-famous eyebrow when they asked if he was secretly engaged to marry one of the ex-wives of a former Rolling Stone, how many pillows he slept on, with whom and how often, what he'd eaten that morning for breakfast.

Consequently, after every performance, the stage door at the rear of the theatre was like Wembley Stadium after a Cup Final.

The women of New York were out to get him, or at least to ogle him up close. Thin ones, fat ones, short ones, tall ones, pretty, young, old, ugly. Every goddamned one of them seemed to be waiting outside the theatre when he tried to sneak out for a smoke. He supposed he should be flattered. He was tired.

He had reached that stage beyond exhaustion where he couldn't even sleep half the time, and that was bad news.

Then he'd seen her. Anna.

Christ no, it couldn't possibly have been Anna! So he'd seen a girl in a plaid wool coat who had long blonde hair and big, round, scared eyes, and his mind had played the familiar trick; his heart had done a double somersault.

It was about time he stopped carrying her around with him everywhere he went, about time he began to enjoy all the razzle-dazzle his growing army of female fans seemed so eager to offer him.

Anna was gone for good, coiled up and locked away in her brave, drab little life, halfway across the world in Pendleton. She wasn't ever coming back to him. It was time he got happy somewhere else.

Otherwise he might as well join a monastery. A liberal monastery where they would accept the fact that he would have to go off and dance now and then because he loved to dance. He could donate his increasingly fat purses to the order, to the Church.

His love had gone with Anna. He didn't want to know.

Nicole, for example. She was pretty, sexy too, very beddable in her Juliet robes, the clinging leotards she wore in the modern stuff. But he didn't want to take her to bed. Hadn't really wanted to that first and only time.

She was still standing there behind him, waiting. Dominic smiled at her reflection in his dressing mirror and offered her a mock-salute.

'I'm sorry, Nicole. I simply can't do it.'

She sighed. 'Okay. I'll save you a drumstick if you want.'

'No thanks. Just enjoy yourself for both of us.'

Dominic removed his make-up, showered, dressed, jostled and smiled and waved his way through the packed plaza and hailed a cab. Food, and then sleep. Alone.

Anna took her seat for the final New York performance of *Romeo and Juliet*.

Tomorrow she would leave, she would go home. But with nothing really resolved, nothing worked out tidily, satisfactorily, *finally*, in her heart.

At least she had been able to cry for him, scalding tears which left their traces in her unquiet heart long after she had dried her eyes; that had happened the morning she saw him, when they were separated only by a sheet of glass when she stared into the restaurant.

She knew then that the love was still there, still as strong as it ever had been, and finding out she had wept again. The love would be there until the day she died. But she had sent Dominic away.

He had found other comfort; fame, adulation. She had

only to glance at an occasional newspaper to realize that.

So she would go home to England, to Pendleton, to shopping in the Co-op on Saturday mornings with her mother, to the life of a small-town ballet mistress with a shadowy, glittering past.

Some day she would have blue-rinsed white hair and be an institution in the town. Children would be carefully taught to say, 'Mornin', Miss Farnell, how're you keeping then?'

Anna tensed. The curtain was rising on the market place in Verona, and Prokofiev's sweeping, symphonic interpretation of Shakespeare's tragic story.

Suddenly all the barriers were down and the real pain began. It kept growing and swelling until it filled Anna's heart and forced its way down her cheeks as scene after scene of the beloved ballet unfolded, as she watched Dominic dancing for the last time.

Anna had never danced Juliet to Dominic's Romeo in performance, though they had rehearsed it many times; it was part of the English Company's repertory, just as was Tchaikovsky's version. This production was the bolder of the two; it was Anna's favourite. She had dreamed of one day dancing it with Dominic.

It was Anna standing in the wings, not Nicole. Anna was worrying over her slipper, convinced it had come undone. She was paralyzed with stage-fright.

Then Anna was on stage; Juliet was smiling sweetly, innocently, as she was introduced to Paris, the wealthy young nobleman who had sought her father's permission to marry her.

Anna danced the ballroom scene in which Romeo was first captivated by Juliet's superbly delicate solo.

She remembered her dream then, the dream of herself on the balcony and Dominic in the garden below. Act I,

Scene 6. Curtain. First Interval. Chaos. The warning bell for Act II. That was it! Then the telephone call from the hotel desk.

It went on like that, an extension of the dream. She knew it so well; she wanted so much to be up there beside him. God, she had known pain, but this was worse than anything that had gone before.

The ballet unfolded eerily, crazily; it was like a reel of film gone wrong, speeded-up and spinning wildly to its brilliant, tragic conclusion.

Act II, Scene 1. The market place. Romeo can think only of Juliet; as a wedding party passes, he dreams of the day he will marry her. Juliet's nurse pushes her way through the crowds in search of Romeo to give him the letter in which Juliet has consented to be his wife.

Act II, Scene 2. The lovers are secretly married by Friar Laurence. Anna and Dominic become man and wife. No, not Anna. Not Dominic.

Kneeling, kneeling so gracefully on the hard boards of the stage for the Friar's blessing; holding one another's glance as he prays for an end to the feud between their two families.

And then Romeo is banished, exiled for avenging the death of his friend Mercutio in a street fight.

The warning bell. The chaos again, the quick, nervous chattering while they waited for the curtain to rise on the last act.

Act III, Scene 1. Her bedroom. It is dawn, and Dominic must go. Romeo embraces Juliet and leaves as her parents enter the room with Paris. Juliet refuses Paris' offer of marriage; he is hurt, and leaves. Her parents are furious with her. Juliet, distraught, rushes to find Friar Laurence.

Scene 2 . . . Scene 3 . . .

She falls at the Friar's feet and pleads for his help. He gives her a sleeping draught; her parents, believing her dead, will bury her in the family tomb. Friar Laurence will warn Romeo, who will return under cover of darkness and take her away from Verona.

And at last Dominic was holding her, Romeo was holding Juliet. So close. Whisper close. He failed to receive the Friar's message and he thought she was dead, and so he drank poison.

Life without one another was unbearable . . . unthinkable, and so when Juliet awoke from her drugged sleep and found him, she stabbed herself. It was so brutally unfair, what the gods had done to her, done . . . to them . . .

When Anna finally stumbled to her feet the theatre was empty.

She would go out to the street, hail a taxi to take her back to the hotel.

One last glimpse of him, just from a safe distance. One farewell glimpse of him, surely that wasn't too much to want. She could take that with her, just that.

Anna left the theatre and walked around it to the rear. She stayed in the shadows behind the mêlée of pushing, shouting women near the stage door.

Dominic was there, at the top of some concrete steps on a little railed landing. He was smiling, shouting good-naturedly at the women to go away and leave him in peace.

Anna looked at him, drinking in one last impression of his beloved face before she turned away forever, hiding behind the seething mass of females who had apparently created a make-believe lover out of the man she had held so many times in her arms.

But now the whole bittersweet, sentimental journey was over.

She started to cry again, and turned away. She walked quickly, murmuring, 'Sorry . . . sorry . . . sorry,' to the handbags and elbows in her ribs as she went.

Dominic sensed rather than saw the moving patch of plaid, the back of a blonde head. When he ran down the steps the mass of women parted, too astonished by his action to grab at him and slow him down.

'Hey! A-n-n-a! Anna, Anna, A-n-n-a-a-a-a!'

Anna ran as fast as she could through the crowd, back to the lights and a taxi, the hotel and the plane back to England, home to a future without him.

'A-n-n-a! Anna, wait for me!'

She heard him running behind her. Nearer and nearer. When he grabbed her arm she stopped still and hung her head. She was still crying, she couldn't help it. She hadn't meant this to happen, she'd only wanted—

He held her shoulders while he studied her face, lovingly, in the dim light; he smiled. 'Anna, stop running, all right?'

Her chin trembled and her eyes brimmed with tears as she smiled back at him.

He took her into his arms, and kissed her hair. She could feel his heart beating against hers.

That was all they needed to begin again.